GOLD AMONGST THE HEATHER

PAUL YOUDEN

PUBLISHED BY MTSTUDIOS

ACKNOWLEDGEMENTS

The Author would like to extend grateful thanks to the following for their kind assistance.

- The Management and staff of Lochs & Glens Holidays
- His Grace, The Duke of Argyll
- The Management and Staff of the Cononish Mine, Tyndrum
- The Manager on The Highland Hotel, Fort William, for his complicity in the story
- The genuine and welcoming people of the Scottish Highlands for their considerable assistance
- Enterprise Car Hire for their considerable help
- Matt Stanley-Webb without whose help this Novel could not have been published

CHAPTER

1

Peter Kingston had spent a month recuperating in the western Highlands of Scotland at the Loch Awe hotel and as his general injuries had healed following the plane crash at Oban airport, he had begun to long to be back in the newspaper office. However, the bullet wound to his head had healed more slowly and the doctors had told him to take things quietly.

Fortunately, as a 32-year-old of average height and generally a very fit young man, it was not long before he had returned to full health and had looked forward to being back at work full time with the cut and thrust of life in a busy newsroom on a county newspaper. Writing had always been in his blood and even at grammar school and then at the Journalist Training College, his prowess with words had shone through.

The time with his wonderful girlfriend, Sue, had proved increasingly therapeutic. It could not easily be described in medical terms as "quiet!" and it was not as though Peter was ungrateful to Sue for being there in his hour of need.

He frequently recalled their nights together in Scotland which had become increasingly passionate once Sue realised Peter's various injuries had healed sufficiently to withstand – and enjoy – deep moments of passion. She was tender, loving and caring and had taken time off herself from her London job to spend time with Peter.

But it had ended all too quickly, the Scottish doctors from Oban hospital had eventually declared him fit for work and now he was back in his newspaper office in Surrey. The snow-capped mountain of the western Highlands was now a distant memory as were the romantic scenes of Loch Awe, the West Highland Railway and the food – especially the food - served mornings and evenings by the hotel staff who had proved thoughtful and caring but remained at arm's length, having learned of Peter's ordeal.

In fact, down south Peter had been national headlines for a few days and a number of journalists from both sides of the border had tried to get Peter to give interviews. Management at the Loch Awe hotel had politely but firmly informed them that Peter Kingston was resting and not prepared to make comments or to give interviews. All information must be got from the Scottish Police.

Peter had agreed to give his own newspaper an exclusive interview over the phone and had created his own headline by outlining all that had happened – or as much as he could recall of the terrible events both in Austria and Switzerland. Details of the plane crash at Oban airport were still sketchy and largely down to what he had been told while recovering in his private room at Oban hospital.

Sue had been given compassionate leave of absence from her own job as a photojournalist on a national magazine in London to spend time with Peter as he recovered. She had twice accompanied him to the hospital at Oban on the West Highland Line which had taken 40 minutes from the Loch Awe hotel to the west coast fishing port and on one occasion one of the hospital's

Consultants had even visited Peter at the Loch Awe hotel using the excuse that too much travelling at an early stage was not good for Peter. Really it was just an excuse to enjoy the scenery and a hearty meal at the hotel.

She had travelled back on the train to London with Peter and their parting, by mutual agreement, at Euston Station, had been warm, clingy but brief. "Let me get settled back into work Sue and we can meet in a week's time and resume where we left off," Peter had told Sue.

He had been welcomed back to his office as a reluctant hero, the newspaperman who had tracked down the notorious international drugs baron who had died in the same plane crash at Oban airport in which Peter had survived, just.

His Editor, Bert Maynard, had put Peter on "light reporting duties" and as acting deputy News editor as it was realised that Peter had a skill for spotting a good news story and getting the best out of work colleagues around him by suggesting leads and angles for the story.

Peter's car which had been parked in the hotel underground car park when he had been kidnapped had been returned to the UK by the AA via an affiliated European breakdown company. The low loader had come across the Channel on a P&O ferry and at Dover the car had been transferred to an AA breakdown truck and taken to Reigate where the local garage had replaced all four tyres. The ones which had been slashed by members of the drugs gang in the underground hotel garage at the ski resort of Lech-am-Arlberg were useless. Peter's car had also been cleaned and serviced. But it held "memories" which were not good ones and Peter decided he would part exchange it at the first opportunity.

Peter's parents – more especially his mother – had welcomed him back with open arms after the dreadful events of the previous few months. His Mother had initially fussed over him more like a mother hen and Peter had reluctantly decided the time had come for him to move out. He needed his own space!

Sue lived in London and that was just too much of a daily commute, so Peter had scanned the properties "vacant" pages and had quickly found himself a first-floor self-contained apartment on the outskirts of Reigate. It was largely furnished and decorated to a high standard, so Peter had little to do once he had convinced his parents, and especially his mother, it was time to "leave the nest". But he had promised to return home – occasionally – for a Sunday family lunch.

Much to his "horror" his original girlfriend, Melissa, who Peter had politely but firmly told back in December that their relationship was over had turned up one day fussing over him. "Oh Peter, I read all about those dreadful things that had happened to you but now that you are back, I can take care of you and help you to fully recover. I have missed you so much!"

Peter had to firmly tell Melissa that he had "moved on". He did not want to hurt her feelings but any relationship they might have once had was now at an end. "I know you mean well Melissa but really, I do not want to be tied down. We are two opposites, and you have to know now it will never work out between us. You are a very sweet, loving girl and you will certainly make someone someday very happy, but it will not be me, Melissa. I am sorry but you just had to know."

Melissa was heartbroken and pleaded with Peter not to rush his decision. "I am not rushing anything Melissa. I made the decision while out in Austria and Switzerland and certainly before those dreadful things had happened to me. I am not sure I am ready to settle down to a married home life with anyone, Melissa. I am so caught up in my work that I do not want any hang-ups at this stage. I am sorry but that is the bottom line".

Peter had thrown himself back into work and as each day passed, he had shown he had a knack of spotting stories and directing the more novice work colleagues on how best to approach difficult and sensitive stories. This had won him the approval of his editor and other senior journalists.

Sundays were always a bit of a drag with his Mother's Sunday lunch. He had twice taken Sue along (somewhat under protest), but he had told Sue that the quicker he and she were accepted as "an item" in the eyes of his mother, the better all-round it would be. His Father was very supportive throughout and did much to smooth the passage with Peter's Mother.

When Peter had an evening off – or better still a Friday and Saturday – he would call up Sue and they would either meet at Sue's London flat or have a couple of nights away at a country inn or small hotel. Their relationship had developed from just being passionate to now being meaningful, but both had agreed not to rush things and certainly not speak of "settling down together". Both agreed it was early days and they would let events take their course.

A couple of months had gone by and one April morning, Peter was unexpectedly summoned to his editor's office. Peter thought he had been performing well so what could possibly have gone wrong? He entered and was invited to sit down.

Bert Maynard looked long and hard at Peter, commented on how well he looked having clearly got over all of his injuries, and said he was impressed with Peter's work in the newsroom.

"Peter, I know you enjoyed your travel writing and were just getting into those winter sports articles when events overtook you. At the time we were not best pleased that you had taken it upon yourself to get too close to those drug smuggling criminals but all of that is in the past. How would you like another shot of producing some more travel articles?"

Well, you could have knocked Peter over with a feather! "What sort of travel articles, would I be sent abroad again," asked Peter.

Bert Maynard immediately retorted. "No way will we be letting you lose into Europe or elsewhere overseas again, well certainly not in the short term. No, a Scottish tour company appear to be offering holidays in the Scottish Highlands which are proving extremely attractive to people here in the south and especially our readership area. You stayed in one of their hotels in the Highlands while you were recovering, and they have particularly expressed a wish for you to write a series of Advertorials – as you know they take paid advertising space and these are accompanied by articles highlighting the merits of such holidays."

Bert Maynard looked at Peter and asked him if he would be interested?

"Yes, I think I most certainly would", replied Peter. "Would this be for a week or longer and would I get a free hand in developing the articles?"

Bert Maynard said obviously the advertorials would have to be written with the tour company in mind and Peter would initially have just six days in the Highlands to produce it. "However, I would like you to find and develop some associated articles about the Western Highlands of Scotland and how these new Scottish Independent people are trying to re-establish Scotland as a separate country from the rest of Britain, who knows, your articles could find a broader market within our newspaper group. So, I think a total of three weeks will allow you sufficient time to have a good hunt round for something along these lines and anything else you come up with. I will expect to hear from you on a daily basis and you can bounce ideas off me," said Bert.

There were other details to be finalised, but Peter was informed his trip to Scotland would take place within the coming week. "The sooner we can provide the travel articles to support the advertising which has been promised the better all rounds. The Holiday Company are anxious to get you up there as soon as possible so that you can see their various hotels and type of operation they run. So, get in touch with their PR and Marketing lady and take it from there," said Bert Maynard.

Peter returned to the newsroom and picked up the phone and was soon connected to Sue. He outlined the news and initially Sue was uncertain. " Peter, Scotland has memories and not all are good. Are you sure you really want to return to the Western Highlands and dredge up those bad memories so early into your recovery?" Peter said he was confident the bad dreams and thoughts were behind him, and, after all, they had together shared some wonderful moments. "Sue, I was wondering if you would be able to get some time off and come with me, either for the first or the second of the two scheduled weeks."

Peter told her he had been given the choice of flying from Gatwick to Glasgow or by taking the train from London to Glasgow. There would be a hire car available for the three weeks. Sue promised to speak to her own editor and phone Peter that evening but somehow Peter felt she was a little "cold" towards him. He dismissed the thoughts as nonsense.

Peter thought the train from London would be more relaxing and he needed to get information on car hire. One of his work colleagues hired cars from time to time and he suggested the company might be prepared to do a deal. He told Peter that if he could mention the Company and car within his travel article, he might get a useful discount!

Peter knew the article about the Scottish Travel firm would be about the total package they offered which was coach-based from various starting points in the south to various hotel destinations throughout the Western Highlands. However, his time at Loch Awe had also shown him that "self-drive packages" were also available and perhaps the Company might allow him to mention this.

So, having gone through the various news items of the day which needed allocating to various journalists, Peter found the phone number of the head office of the car hire company and put in a call.

Having asked for the press or PR department, he was finally connected to a lady and he outlined what the purpose of his forthcoming trip to Scotland was about. The lady asked if he could email her with details and she would run it past her manager and get back to Peter by the end of the day.

As Peter put down the phone the other Newsroom phone on Peter's desk rang and picking it up he learned there had been a smash-and-grab raid on a local High street jewellers' shop in Reigate in which guns had been produced. Nobody had been injured but two female shop assistants were suffering from shock. The whole area had been cordoned off by police.

Peter immediately turned on his swivel chair, called across to Jeremy who was one of the senior writers and asked him to drop whatever he was doing and get down to the High Street. "This is so out-of-character for Reigate and it may just be opportunist local criminals or it could be a London gang out for a soft touch in the provinces. See what you can gleam from one of the senior detectives," said Peter.

Jeremy left taking one of the junior reporters. "There will be some leg work involved and this will help you to get your teeth into something more interesting than flower and baby shows," Jeremy told the young reporter.

Having satisfied himself the urgent news story was in capable hands; Peter next phoned the Scottish Holiday Company and asked to be put through to the PR/Marketing lady. "Alison speaking," said a very matter-of-fact female voice. Peter introduced himself and immediately he detected a warm change of voice from the other end.

"Ah, Peter Kingston. Yes, you are coming up to write some marketing articles for your newspaper group which we are going to support with advertising. I am looking forward to meeting you." Peter asked why the holiday company had specifically requested him. "You are the young man who recovered at our Loch Awe hotel having been pulled from the wreckage of that dreadful plane crash at Oban airport. I took a particular interest in hearing all about the dreadful things which had happened to you. And I believe you are just the bright young newspaper person who can portray our Company in the way we would like to be seen by your readers down south," said Alison.

Peter informed Alison his Editor had indicated he could be released from his current newsroom duties in the coming days. "That sounds perfect," said Alison. "Saturday is our switch over day with new guests arriving by coach around teatime. Could you meet me at our flagship hotel at Ardgartan on Loch Long around 3pm for a coffee and chat," she asked.

Peter explained his travel plans. "I know you offer Self Drive so I thought I would incorporate that within my articles although I will mainly feature the coach holiday side of your business. Will that be OK," Alison said it would be fine and Peter asked Alison to email him directions from Glasgow Airport as that was where he would be getting his hire car from.

Peter's desk phone rang. It was the lady from the car rental company. "I have run your idea past my manager and he has agreed to give you a special deal. You will just cover the insurance and fuel used so I hope that is OK?" she asked.

That is fine by me and I am sure my Editor will be delighted commented Peter." Can I pick the car up by lunchtime on Saturday from Glasgow?" asked Peter. The lady said they could do better than that. "Just let me know what time your train will arrive at Glasgow Central station and we will have a car and driver collects you. He will take you to our office at Glasgow Airport so that you can quickly complete the paperwork and then, off you go."

Peter said it all sounded great and he would ensure she had the details in the next 24 hours.

Back to the here and now Peter knocked at Bert Maynard's door and asked if his editor had a few minutes to spare. The answer was a "Yes, but be quick please!"

Peter outlined his travel plans including arrangements with the car hire and his arrival on Saturday afternoon at the Lochs and Glens Ardgartan hotel. Bert said he was pleased with what Peter had achieved.

Next were the events of the day. The smash and grab where only gold items had been taken. Peter told Bert that this alone made him suspicious the raid had been carefully planned as gold was currently commanding such a high price on the world market, especially in former eastern bloc countries.

Bert and Peter both agreed it was front page news and Peter started sketching out ideas on his desktop computer. A photo of the shop; perhaps a photo of some similar gold items and any photo-fit pictures of the criminals the police might issue.

Next, Peter used his mobile to call his reporter – Jeremy. "Any updates on the value of the haul; any photo-fit pictures being issued by the police; any signs of the car used for the getaway?" asked Peter. Jeremy said he would shortly be returning to the office to write his article but he could reveal the getaway car had been found 3 miles away minus the gang and the haul of gold items.

Peter told him it was to be front page news for the next day's paper and a separate story on the state of the two women jewellery shop assistants with a photo would be run. "That should please our up-and-coming young reporter," Peter told Jeremy.

Within the next hours the front-page story was taking shape. The value of the haul had been put at a staggering half a million and it turned out this was the latest in a series of raids across the Home Counties. The police believed the same eastern European gang was involved but there were no definite identi-fit photos. The two shop assistant ladies had said the gang's faces had been masked and they had been so shocked by the sight of the guns they had been too stressed to take more notice.

By 7pm that evening the front page was prepared and ready for Bert Maynard's approval. Photos of the two women; a photo of the abandoned getaway car; a photo of the jewellery ship and a smaller photo of similar gold items to some of those stolen in the robbery made a captivating front page.

Peter liked Jeremy's write up. He also thought the account of the two women shop assistants written by the young reporter had promise and he told him so. He also mentioned to Bert Maynard that Jeremy might "hold the fort" as acting news editor while he was in Scotland. Bert thought the suggestion had merit.

That evening back at his flat Peter started to prepare clothing for his few weeks in Scotland. Springtime so it should not be too cold and although he would be staying in various Lochs and Glens hotels, he did not think he would need a suit. Just smart casual should suffice. Peter phoned Sue. No reply and that was unusual. Just a voicemail asking callers to leave a message so Peter asked Sue to phone back that evening as tomorrow was Friday and Peter would be leaving from London early Saturday morning.

Next he decided to phone home and inform his parents he was off to Scotland. As usual his Mother thought he should spend more time in Surrey recovering before setting off on travels again but Peter's Father was his usual supportive self and said they would look forward to reading the first of Peter's Scottish articles.

Peter again phoned Sue but still it was an answerphone. Most unusual but perhaps some work commitment had come up!

There was a lot of packing to do; which clothes to take and be prepared for all types of Scottish weather despite it being springtime. Next, he went online and booked his Euston to Glasgow ticket for Saturday morning. He selected the 07.30 departure noting there would be only five stops and a scheduled journey time of just four and a half hours. He remembered to reserve a seat; by a window and forward facing and arranged to collect the tickets at the train desk at Euston.

Eventually his phone in the flat rang. It was nearly 11pm and it was Sue. "I am sorry Peter, something came up at work and I had to rush out. The assignment took longer than expected." But there was something in her voice which did not sound the usual "her". Peter told Sue "no worries" but as he would be leaving early on Saturday morning from Euston he wondered if he could spend Friday night at her London flat.

"Yes, that's fine" said Sue. "But the bad news is I cannot get any leave for at least a week, maybe ten days, so you will have to do the first part of Scotland alone," she said.

Peter's heart sank but he disguised his disappointment down the phone by trying to sound cheerful and said he was looking forward to seeing her the following day. "Shall we have dinner out," he asked. Sue said she would prefer to cook something at the flat. "That will give us longer time to relax together," said Sue.

The next morning Peter's day at the office started early. The newspaper was published and the front page looked really good. There had been no police developments overnight and the robbery had even got a mention on national news.

The weekly newsroom meeting was headed by Bert Maynard who said the paper looked good and he was pleased with everyone's efforts. He also said Peter would be doing a series of articles from Scotland over the next three weeks so Jeremy would be "acting news editor". He reminded Peter that a daily "keep in touch" phone call would be expected. There were a few chuckles around the room and Peter smiled. Not much chance of getting into trouble in the wilds of the Scottish Highlands!

Peter's day was soon over and having loaded his case and laptop into the car, he headed off to Sue's London flat, arriving at 6.30pm having had a fairly easy journey with rush hour traffic heading in the opposite direction out of London.

Sue greeted Peter with apparent warm affection. Dinner would be ready about 8pm so why not a nice hot shower and then a cuddle on the sofa" suggested Sue. "I have a better idea. Why not an affectionate or even passionate embrace in bed and then a shower while you serve the meal," Peter chuckled and winked. Sue responded by unexpectedly agreeing saying "It could be our last for a week or ten days so we had better make the most of it!"

It was warm, passionate and meaningful. Sue's slim body, already rid of her bra and pants, slid between the sheets and lay next to Peter's already aroused and naked body. It had been over a week since they had last made love and this was not sex simply for the sake of sex, it was passionate love making between two people who felt they meant so much to each other. Peter's hands had gently caressed her smooth skin from her neck down to her waist; Peter knew the areas of Sue's body that were easily aroused and she gently groaned as his hand slid down her inner thigh. Sue had responded by entwining her long slim legs around Peter's finally encouraging him on top. He had tenderly caressed her firm breasts before his tongue found her firm nipples. This had brought squeals of rapture from Sue and she pleaded with Peter." Please, oh please Peter. Don't wait, make love to me now and he had, surprising himself how quickly they had each climaxed at the same time. Both lay back exhausted.

Twenty minutes later Sue said she had to finish the cooking and Peter said he would have his shower. Nothing else was said until they sat down for a lovely meal of Brixham crab layered with cheese and grilled. What a yummy starter. Next came a ribeye steak with diced roast baby potatoes and a stir fry mixture of vegetables. The dessert was yoghurt-based fruit salad and Peter said the whole meal, washed down with a Malbec red wine was so tasty and filling he could not eat the cheese course which Sue said was available if he was still hungry!

Sue and Peter spent an hour on the sofa talking about his plans for Scotland. "I hope I might be able to join you halfway through your second week, Peter, but my magazine is so busy my editor says there is no way I can be given time off any sooner," said Sue. Peter asked her if there was anything on her mind. "Why do you ask that" responded Sue with an edge to her voice. "No reason, Sue, other than you have appeared at times recently not to be so fully committed to "us". Sue retorted she felt Peter was being silly. "It is just I have a lot of work things on my mind."

Peter had brought with him a copy of his newspaper and having read the front-page article Sue remarked about the type of robbery.

"You know Peter. I tend to agree with you as most jewellery shop thieves would have gone for diamond rings, bracelets and diamond earrings. Just to focus on gold items is certainly unusual," said Sue.

Peter's comment was a simple one.

"And I thought diamonds were a girl's best friend." But Sue retorted. "I think I could be satisfied by gold!"

CHAPTER

2

Peter's train journey on that Saturday morning had been uneventful. His tickets had been waiting for him at Euston as promised. His reserved seat was in the next carriage to the buffet car towards the front of the 12-carriage train and so he had enjoyed a railway breakfast of fresh orange juice, yoghurt, and a banana. He had left Sue in bed as the taxi he had ordered the evening before had arrived promptly at 6.30am. His car would be safe at Sue's and she had promised to keep an eye on it. His journey from west London to Euston had been easy on that quiet Saturday morning.

Now as the miles sped by Peter was able to concentrate on the task ahead. Warrington, Wigan, Preston and Carlisle stations had been and gone. The train had crossed into Scotland without anyone really noticing. The Train Manager had announced they were on time and would be arriving at Glasgow at 12.10. Peter phoned the car rental firm and they assured him the car and driver would be there waiting.

Great!

Peter had plugged in his laptop during the train journey and had Googled

Lochs and Glens Holidays to get background information on how long the company had been running. He had studied the various hotels and also looked at different itineraries which were available to holidaymakers at different times of the year. Everything was included and the holidays looked excellent value. Accommodation rated at 3*; an extensive breakfast and equally mouth-watering choice of evening cuisine plus entertainment at each hotel every evening and coach tours out each day. Amazing, thought Peter.

Soon he was at Glasgow, down the platform and at the ticket barrier was a young lady waving a large card with Peters name on it. "Hi, I am Peter Kingston", he said as he shook the young lady's hand. She introduced herself as Fiona and he guessed she was mid-twenties with flaxen-coloured hair and a petit figure beneath the jacket and smart black very feminine trousers.

"How well do you know Scotland Mr Kingston?" asked Fiona? "Well firstly I would prefer it if you called me Peter, secondly it is a bit of a long story but I spent a month in the Highlands at Loch Awe recovering from a bit of a plane crash but apart from views from my hotel windows, I did not get to see too much of the country," he said.

As Fiona drove through the Glasgow city traffic and out via the Clyde tunnel and onto the M74 south of Scotland's capital, Fiona glanced across at Peter and said. "It has just clicked. I read all about you earlier this year in the Glasgow Herald. You were mixed up with an international drug smuggling gang and got shot in the head. Am I right?"

Peter was quite surprised. "Well, yes in a way but I was never part of any drug smuggling gang. I just happened to be in the wrong place at the wrong time and I knew nothing about the plane crash at Oban airport until I came to in the Oban hospital. I try not to think about it as the memories of burns and the head wound still give me bad dreams," said Peter. "Now I am back to write all about your idyllic western Highlands and the reasons why people from down south should spend more of their holidays here in Scotland," he said.

Within twenty minutes they had arrived at the car rental office at Glasgow airport. Peter had not realised what a busy airport it was. Various airlines were based here and international flights from Scandinavia to America, scheduled flights from London and other UK airports to charter holiday flights. It was certainly busy.

The paperwork was ready. It just needed a few signatures from Peter including his responsibility for any speeding and other traffic violations and £100 damage insurance. Peter asked how long the journey from the airport to Loch Long and the Ardgartan hotel would take. Fiona told him he needed to head over the Erskine Bridge and then Loch Lomond.

"I could even show you Peter because coincidentally I live at the nearby village of Tarbet and I have the rest of the weekend off. I am not due back here at the office until Monday lunchtime and my Mother can drive me in," said Fiona. "But of course I do not want to appear pushy and if you prefer not, then it is no problem!"

Peter thought it would be a splendid idea. Her company and the chance to get to know this rather attractive Scottish lass, he thought to himself! "I have an appointment with the marketing lady of Lochs and Glens at 4pm today and I will be staying at the Ardgartan hotel at least two nights so how about dinner at the hotel tomorrow evening, we could provisionally say 6pm for pre-dinner drinks and I will see what time the hotel can do dinner for two?"

Fiona said that sounded very nice, so Peter gave her his mobile phone number and asked her to call him either later that evening or the following day as he was not too sure what itinerary they had put together for him.

Their drive from the airport up the side of Loch Lomond had been remarkably pleasant with Fiona pointing out various landmarks and remarking that Loch Lomond was reputed to be the largest Loch in the UK. It had taken about an hour for the drive and soon they were at the small village of Tarbet. Before getting out at her parent's small 3-bedroomed house, Fiona gave Peter directions on how to find the Ardgartan hotel. "It is no more than 10 minutes from here. Follow this road, you will come to Loch Long and just follow the road around the top end of the Loch. On the far side the road begins to climb but just before the snow gates you will see a sign near a bus shelter on the left saying Ardgartan hotel – Lochs and Glens. Turn off and a small, winding road takes you through the wood to the large, impressive hotel," she said.

Peter thanked Fiona who got out, waved and called..." I'll phone you later Peter" and she disappeared towards the house without turning back.

Peter arrived at the Ardgartan hotel and went in with his suitcase and laptop. Within minutes a receptionist appeared from a back room and said, "Yes, may I help". She had a foreign accent!

Peter introduced himself and said he was a guest invited by Lochs and Glens Holidays and would be meeting their Marketing/PR lady – Alison – who should be arriving shortly. He was reassured when the lady smiled and said he was expected. Alison had phoned to say she was on her way and would be at the hotel in the next 20 minutes. "I will show you to your room, but please do not worry about your case as one of our staff will bring it up," she said. Peter discreetly looked at her name badge of her chest and noted it was Gisela. As they made their way to the first floor in the lift Peter had noted the high standard of the reception area, the wall-to-wall carpeting, leather sofa and armchairs and the huge glass windows which gave a magnificent view down Loch Long.

"You are not British," remarked Peter casually as they stepped out of the lift. "No I am from Poland but I have been here already for two years working for Lochs and Glens Holiday. It is an excellent company to work for and at least half of our staff come from either my country or other European countries," said Gisela.

Peter's room was large; a double and a single bed with two large windows offering fantastic views down the loch. The ensuite was finished to a very high spec with a deep bath and shower over the top; TV, a telephone and tea/coffee making facilities. What more could he ask for. There was a knock at the door and a man delivered Peter's suitcase. He was introduced as another "Peter" but with a different spelling: "Pieter".

Gisela asked to be excused as she must get back to Reception. "Today is change over day and we have four coaches arriving, they are 55 seaters and although they are not all completely full I have over 200 guests to check in," and with that she was gone.

Peter was starting to unpack his toilet things in the bathroom when the phone rang. It was Gisela announcing the Marketing lady from the Holiday firm had arrived and would Peter like tea or coffee in the lounge. Peter thought tea would be great and told her he would be right down.

Alison was waiting by one of the large deep brown leather sofas facing the views of the sun-kissed still waters of Loch Long. There was a tray of tea, some biscuits and a cup of coffee. As Peter approached, Alison turned, smiled and held out her hand. "Welcome Peter; welcome to Ardgartan hotel. Do have a seat and we can enjoy a warm drink while we chat about the articles you are going to write on our behalf," said Alison.

Peter had quickly weighed up this very matter-of-fact lady; smartly dressed and he guessed in her late forties of perhaps early 50's. He was not very good at guessing the age of a woman! Here was a lady with obvious confidence but not Scottish. As Peter sat down and was handed his cup of tea, he remarked on her English accent. "Yes, you are quite right. I am originally from the south of England but many years ago I met and married a Scottish man and came to live in Scotland, just at the time when Lochs and Glens were starting with the first of its hotels," said Alison. "But enough about me as we can chat about personal things over dinner when my husband will be joining us."

Alison outlined why they had decided to do editorially supported advertising and why they had chosen Peter to write for them. "Our business comes from all parts of the UK," said Alison "But the south including London and the Home Counties is an extremely important part of our business and we want to encourage even more people to come and view what Scotland has to offer. You obviously came to our attention during your recuperation at our Loch Awe hotel and we have followed your writing career since you returned to Surrey. We feel you can deliver the sort of interesting and colourful articles we are looking for. Of course, we will allow you as free a hand as you need, bearing in mind we as a Company will be paying for the Advertorial," she said and gave a warm smile.

Peter said he was impressed with what he had seen so far of the Ardgartan hotel." I will give you a short tour in a while but first I would like to outline the plans I have provisionally made for you during the coming week. As you know the coaches take our clients out to various destinations each day and all of this is included in the price of the holiday. Depending on which our hotels people stay at depends on which daily tour. We go on the ferry to Mull and Iona from this and the Loch Awe hotels; Our Loch Achray hotel includes Stirling and Glasgow while the Highland Hotel at Fort William includes tours to Loch Ness and the east coast fishing port of Mallaig. This last one is interesting as it is a one-way train journey on the famous Jacobite steam train – the train used in the Harry Potter films – and our coaches drive out empty to bring clients back"

"Wow", said Peter. "Such a choice and I can imagine different people choosing a particular hotel just because of the itinerary." Alison said it was even more interesting because whilst clients had their particular favourite hotel, they also booked several trips each year just to sample the various different places.

She produced an information pack. "It contains all that I have told you and much, much more as well so this is something for you to look at before we meet for dinner here at 7.30pm I live just across the other side of the water – look, you can see my home over there," said Alison and she pointed to a house on the far shore. "I am a ten-minute drive away so we will now do a short tour of the hotel and you can formulate questions for later.

Alison explained the Ardgartan hotel had only been recently built at a cost of £11m including the nearby building where the staff lived. "We recruit about 60 per cent of our staff from overseas, not always out of choice, but we find it difficult – as do other Scottish hotel groups – to find enough Scottish young people interested in working in the hotel and catering industry," she said.

Together they looked at the large dining room which seated over 200 people. We vary meal times so some days passengers from a particular coach tour will have an early breakfast and early evening meal; the next day it might reverse to later breakfast and evening meal. It means people get personal attention as groups are smaller and more manageable for our staff," said Alison. Next, they looked at the bar, lounge and dance area. Alison collected several room keys from Reception and said she would show Peter various rooms. Nothing to hide and you will see all rooms are finished to a high standard. We try and put our less able-bodied clients on the ground floor, and we do try and give people the type of room they have requested. But not everyone can have a room with a loch view!" she commented.

It was soon time for her to go and Peter returned to his room to study his press pack. He also wanted to phone Sue to let her know he had arrived safely.

Eventually he got an answer from her mobile. "Hi Sue, it's Peter and I am here, and I am very impressed with the hotel." The reaction was not quite what he had been expecting. Sue sounded cold! "I am pleased your journey went well and you are at the hotel. I am sure you will have an interesting time. But I have something to tell you which I did not want to share before you left. I wanted our moments together to be memorable," said Sue.

Peter was frozen to the chair. What on earth was coming next!

"I have been offered a photographic job in New York on a big American magazine and I have decided to accept," said Sue. Before Peter could utter anything, Sue continued "Peter, this is a chance of a lifetime and I know you will be upset, probably angry but we both agreed we did not want to settle down yet. You have your writing career, and this one-year initial contract will open doors for me. You will remain close and dear in my heart, Peter, but perhaps we need a break to see how much we really need each other".

It was an understatement to say he was angry. He felt betrayed. Why could she not have discussed this with him on Friday at her flat? "This is dreadful news Sue and it is like a bolt out of the blue. Yes I am angry, very angry as I thought we had something special between us. I need time to think Sue. When does your new job start?" he asked.

Sue had to some extent prepared herself for Peter's reaction. "I have only been seriously discussing this for the past week and two days ago with my own editor. He is prepared to give me leave of absence for 12 months so I have to consider agreeing to a contract of only a year otherwise my job here in London will not be kept open. I must let the New York magazine have my answer on Monday" she said.

Peter said he was too upset and angry to continue the conversation. "Can we speak tomorrow early evening when I have had time to consider our future," he asked. Sue agreed and said she still had "feelings" for Peter. "I just need space to consider what sort of future I want," she said.

There was nothing further to say and the phone went dead. Peter stood, fixed to the spot holding the bedroom table in his hand. How could she do this to him, it was a betrayal after all they had gone through together – all she had said over recent months. Something had been going on behind the scenes which Sue had not been prepared to share with him. No grounds for a future relationship, he thought!

Peter finished his unpacking, had a shower and prepared for dinner with Alison and her husband. He read through the information in his press pack, considering how he would spend his Sunday and Monday.

Down at Reception Peter was amazed that four coaches could have arrived and guests and luggage all in bedrooms. In fact, Alison had arranged they would be joining the "first sitting" at 7.30pm so he made sure he was early.

Alison arrived and introduced her husband, Fred. He was a true Scot with a broad accent. She asked Peter if he would like a drink in the bar before the meal, but it was agreed a bottle of wine (and a jug of water) at the table would be preferable.

Their table was by one of the many restaurant windows offering great views down Loch Long. Dusk had set in, and Peter could no longer see to the opposite side of the Loch. However, in the distance was a bright orange glow so Peter asked Alison to explain.

"There is a large oil installation down there as well as a NATO naval base. Obviously, security is essential and in addition to large "Out-of-Bounds" areas with round the clock military patrols there is considerable shipping activity as that part of Loch Long joins the river Clyde near Greenock," said Alison.

Peter looked at the dinner menu. He was surprised about the choice. There were four different starters, five mains (including a vegetarian) and four various desserts including ice cream and cheese and biscuits.

Alison explained that they tried to cater for all tastes and appetites. Peter was impressed yet again.

The wine waiter appeared, and Peter expressed a preference for a red. A Chilean Merlot was his favourite. Fred said he also liked red, and the Merlot would be fine. "Although we live just across the other side of the Loch I am driving and I do not drink and drive so I will be sticking to fruit juice and water," said Alison.

Next a waitress appeared and took their order for starters. Peter selected Scottish prawns.

Shortly afterwards a different waiter appeared to take the order for the mains. "Do not look alarmed Peter. It is our system to ensure guests have their food served hot and it also gives our team in the kitchen time to prepare. At this sitting we are serving 116 meals as we also have a few self-drive guests," explained Alison.

While they were waiting Alison asked if Peter had looked through his information pack. He said he had and was impressed by the various itineraries and the many places to visit. Alison said if Peter did not mind she would suggest he used his car the next day to take in the small town of Inveraray on Loch Fyne "There is a very interesting castle there open to the public but it is also the residence of the Duke and Duchess of Argyll," she said.

"After that you could drive to the village of Tyndrum which has an interesting shop and café known as the Green Wellie. Gold has also been discovered in one of the nearby mountains and an Australian mining company has been given mineral rights. The Company is a Scottish subsidiary of the Australian parent firm and have lead mining links in Scotland. However, there is a storm of protest about extraction at Tyndrum as the spoil would be dumped in what is a designated area of outstanding natural beauty," she said. Peter thought this was interesting in itself and would probably make a separate article which his Editor had asked him to look for during his extra weeks in Scotland.

Their starters arrived so conversation switched to enjoying some food and a glass of wine. While plates were being cleared and they waited for their mains Alison said if Peter continued down the road from Tyndrum he would come to Callander, a quaint little town well worth a visit and nearby is our Loch Achray hotel. "I could arrange for you to move to this on Tuesday and spend two days there before moving onto another of our hotels at Fort William if you like," suggested Alison. On this trip you could have a short cruise on the famous Loch Lomond as my husband, Fred, owns and runs the cruises. Fred said it would be a pleasure and he would probably pilot the cruise boat himself. He gave Peter a card and Peter promised to agree times in a phone call the next day.

The mains arrived. Peter had gone for steak and ale pie, a choice also selected by Fred. Alison had chosen a chicken salad explaining she was not a big eater in the evenings.

Another glass of red wine was poured and their conversation centred on life in general in Scotland. Peter was interested in the vote for Independence. Alison said the majority of Scottish people did not favour such a move. "We would like more self-determination such as raising taxes and how we spend the money but it is still felt we are part of the United Kingdom and that is the way it should remain."

The main meal was delicious. "Our chefs in the various hotels are carefully chosen and we try and ensure the same high standard of food is served at all of our six hotels," said Alison. Budgets are set and hotel managers have a strict budget to adhere to. Chefs are allowed a little leeway but generally speaking we try and ensure that if steak and ale pie is on the menu here, at some time during a week it is also on the menu at our other hotels. We arrange central purchasing which helps to keep costs down."

Peter said he had noticed quite a few of the hotel staff came from overseas. "Yes, we employ staff from other European countries. I must emphasise we do try and fill as many vacancies as possible from within Scotland and other parts of the UK but there seems a reluctance of British young people to work in the hotel and catering business. We have serious concerns about the effects of Brexit and the future employment of staff from other parts of Europe," she said. "Our staff has to be flexible and undertake different duties at various times. For example, our waiters also help to load and unload baggage on coach change over days. We could not possibly just have a team of porters standing around kicking their heals for five or six days waiting for the next change of clients," she smiled.

Their desserts came and went. The bottle of red was finished but both Peter and Fred had also enjoyed fresh Scottish water during the meal. Alison asked Peter if there was anything else he wanted to ask. "Fred and I enjoy yachting (we have our own small yacht) and we are planning an early start and a day's sailing down Loch Long to The Clyde and back so if you will excuse us, it is time to go. Also, our staff are preparing for the next guests for their evening meal."

They rose and wandered out to the huge Reception area. Alison and Fred said their "goodnights" and having given Peter both her mobile and office phone number she said he could call if he had any further questions. "But tomorrow is really my day of leisure, but I am sure our Reception staff here at the hotel will be able to help with most questions," said Alison.

Peter thanked them both for an interesting and excellent evening.

With that they were gone, and Peter helped himself to a coffee which all guests were offered in the lounge after their evening meal. He sat down staring down Loch Long contemplating his future – a future perhaps without Sue.

He was devastated and knew he would have a troubled night's sleep!

CHAPTER

3

Peter went to his room, contemplating everything that had happened. He decided on a bit of a long shot and phoned Fiona. "Hi Fiona, it is Peter from the Ardgartan hotel. I hope I am not phoning too late or sounding forward but just wanted to check everything is OK for dinner tomorrow evening."

Fiona said it was lovely to hear from him. "Oh yes, Peter, I am looking forward to our evening and finding out more about you. Have you met with the hotel people, and have you got an itinerary for the coming week," she asked.

"Yes, I have been given quite a free hand and various ideas for the coming day. For example, as tomorrow is Sunday, I was thinking of either visiting Inveraray Castle or taking a look at Aberfoyle and then going on to the Loch Achray hotel near Callander. I suppose it would be really silly of me to ask if you fancy a day out. After all I am sure you would want to spend it at home?"

On the contrary," said Fiona. "I would love a day out and will leave the choice of where you want to take me to you. Strange as it seems I have never been to Inveraray Castle and neither have I seen the Loch Achray hotel. But I do know there is a lake close by with a steam driven pleasure boat and Queen Victoria once stayed nearby."

Gosh, thought Peter. This area is steeped in history, and it would be fun to have Fiona along and help fill in many gaps with her local knowledge.

"OK, that's settled then. Would 10am be ok as I am down for an 8.30am breakfast? It will give me time to gather my thoughts," said Peter.

He got ready for bed and not long after his head had hit the pillow he fell into a surprisingly deep, contented sleep - perhaps a new lady had entered his somewhat shattered life?

Peter woke with mixed thoughts. If his girlfriend, Sue, really wanted her own life back, why could she not have been open enough to tell him to his face. As he washed and got ready for breakfast he reflected on the task at hand. He was in Scotland to do a writing job and this was first and foremost now. Perhaps his day with this new young lady, Fiona, would take his mind off other matters.

He had looked out of the window to see some blue sky and wispy cloud. No rain and very little breeze. Could be a lovely day he thought to himself. He switched on the TV just in time to catch the local forecast for the Highlands. Rain on the way for tomorrow with strengthening winds. "Oh great!" he thought.

He came down to find an entire coach party group were already being served their starters. He was shown to a small table by the window which once again offered great views down Loch Long. He ordered tea, porridge and then scrambled eggs and smoked salmon. Everything arrived hot and was nicely presented by smartly dressed hotel staff.

Peter returned to his room and gathered up his information folder, a small Nikon camera and a road map of the western Highlands. Down at Reception Peter said he would have a guest for dinner that evening and hoped it would be ok. He was asked if he could join the 7.30 sitting and he thought that would be ok. He then phoned Fiona to say he was about to leave Ardgartan and was it still ok to pick her up at her parent's cottage. Fiona confirmed she was ready and looking forward very much to the day out with Peter.

She was waiting by the front gate with a beaming smile as Peter pulled up. "Hi Peter, I hope you slept well in our clean Scottish air," said Fiona. Peter gave her a peck on the cheek as she sat beside him and smiled. He told her his hotel room was first rate and the bed very comfortable. He also said he had booked dinner back at Ardgartan for 7.30 and hoped that was ok. Fiona said it would be a perfect end to the day.

Before they set out Peter said he had studied the map and felt they should head back past the Ardgartan hotel and to Inveraray and spend the morning visiting the castle. "We should make the most of the dry, bright weather as the TV forecast is for it to change overnight" remarked Peter. "If you like we can visit Loch Achray this afternoon and have a coffee and sticky bun on the way so that we are hungry and will enjoy our meal at Ardgartan this evening," he said to Fiona.

It was 10.45 when they pulled up at the castle gates and Peter paid for the two of them. Having parked they made their way to the castle's front door; Peter had taken her hand and she had not pulled it away. Peter had been stunned by the beauty of Inveraray Castle. "It is like something magical from a Disney film," he said to Fiona.

Once inside they were amazed at the armoury and collection of swords, muskets and other medieval weapons of a bygone age. As they moved from room to room looking at the portraits of former Dukes of Argyll and learning some of the castle's history and that of the "military" family they came across a glass cabinet with photos of the current Duke and Duchess as well as their ceremonial robes. Even Fiona who until now had remained somewhat non-committal was "wowed" by the elegance and opulence of the majestic ermine and cloth.

Venturing downstairs, they came first to what had once been the castle's kitchen and washroom. Following signs to the café and shop they walked along a fairly narrow passage and entered a well-stocked shop. Behind the counter was a youngish-looking man in a white shirt, slacks but wearing what looked like a professional painters' apron. "Good morning," he said to both Peter and Fiona.

"Is this your first visit to the castle and is there anything I can help you with." Peter thought his smile genuine and welcoming so Peter then introduced himself as a journalist from down south in Scotland to write a series of travel articles. "In that case you should have contacted my secretary, and we could have arranged a conducted tour. If you have half an hour to spare now then perhaps you will join me for a tea and a chat."

Peter was at first taken aback. "My Castle!" A drink and a chat; Peter thought he must be imagining things but then came the surprise. "I am sorry; I should have introduced myself properly. You see I am the Duke and I often help here in the shop. It is usually my wife's domain, but she is busy with our three young children who are home from boarding school in London. They are always hungry so my wife is preparing their favourite Sunday roast."

Peter was astounded. Fiona could not believe that here she was, out with a young journalist, visiting Inveraray Castle for the first time not a million miles from her Scottish home and she gets to meet a real life "Duke". She did not know whether to curtsey; break out in a cold sweat or just crumble to the floor.

The Duke then spoke to a female member of staff serving at the far end of the shop counter. Peter heard, "Yes, certainly Your Grace" before they were led from the room, back up to the ground floor where the Duke produced a huge cast-iron key from his overalls, put it into an equally huge mortice lock and they found themselves in the Duke and Duchess's private quarters.

Having been invited to sit in the private lounge, The Duke disappeared but returned after ten minutes with a tray of tea and biscuits. "I hope you do not mind but I took it upon myself as it is one of my favourites to make you a pot of Earl Grey." Biscuits are optional, he remarked with a smile!

"Now tell me about this writing and how or if I can help," said The Duke.

Peter explained the main purpose of the visit, to write a paid-for editorial covering two pages about Lochs and Glens but also to include places of interest where coach passengers could visit.

"But I will be staying on for a further two weeks to write my own travel articles about Scotland and especially the Western Highlands. I am sure there are many places waiting to be discovered by those from "down south" and what I have seen of this lovely country in the past twenty-four hours has already impressed me and given me a lot of food for thought," said Peter.

The Duke asked Peter what he did back at the newspaper and having explained in general, Peter told the story of the smash and grab raid which had happened in Reigate the previous week. "The strange thing is the thieves only went for items of gold such as rings, bracelets, high-end watches and necklaces. Diamonds were purposely left behind."

"Peter, do you know we have our own gold here in Scotland? Just last year a huge gold seam was discovered just up the road at a small village called Tyndrum and with current gold prices it could already be worth £100 million," said The Duke.

"Wow" remarked Fiona which brought a warm smile from The Duke.

"Wow indeed," said Peter. "So is this gold deposit on the Argyll Estate?" asked Peter.

"Unfortunately not, well as far as I know. Geological surveys are very expensive and to date there are no indications the Tyndrum gold seams extend this far. If only, I might be sunning myself and the family on some Caribbean island," he said with a chuckle.

Over a second cup of tea they chatted some more about the Castle and its history and Peter asked The Duke if he would be prepared to meet again for a more detailed chat for another of Peter's articles.

"Certainly," said The Duke. Give my secretary a call and she can find a date and time in the next ten days when we can chat for longer. Now I really must join the family and then go back down to the shop. Sundays is always busy for us at the Castle".

Peter and Fiona were taken back to the public part of the Castle and thanked The Duke of Argyll for his time and the lovely, warm welcome and chat. "I look forward to our next meeting," said The Duke. "Me too your Grace," said Peter.

Back at the car, Peter and Fiona sat and deliberated for a few minutes." That was really so very interesting and worthwhile," said Peter. Fiona said she could never have dreamed in a hundred years of ever having the chance to meet a real live Duke. "I have only known you a few hours and already my life is more interesting. What other goodies have you in store for me, Peter", she asked.

Peter looked at her for a few minutes and felt a warm glow. Here was a lovely, down to earth but very attractive young lady who had suddenly come into his life like a breath of Scottish fresh air.

"I have nothing definite in mind right at this moment, but I'll work on some idea," he said with a chuckle. Fiona smiled back and said whatever it was she would look forward to it!

Having studied the road map Peter said it might be a good idea to drive from Inveraray to the village of Tyndrum. "It might give me the chance to ask in local shops what the villagers think of being part of the gold-mining village," he said.

They set off and within forty minutes they were there. "That was breathtaking scenery on the way," remarked Peter. "I would love to do that journey again during the coming week." Fiona said if only she could join him. "Work on it back at your office then," he said.

They pulled into the village store car park. "Give me a minute or two to ask a few questions and I'll be right back," said Peter. Fiona sat in the car watching cars, coaches and trucks passing through on their way to Rannoch Moor, Glencoe and the road to Fort William. She thought to herself, "I had no idea how busy roads through the Highlands are. I must spend too much time in and around Glasgow!"

Peter was soon back. "Not a very good welcome. Most of the villagers are not welcoming the idea of a gold mine on their doorstep and not even the prospect of lots more business and tourism seems to sway any argument. They seem to feel their community will be changed forever once gold mining really gets underway," said Peter to Fiona.

Just down the road was a large service station with café and shop called The Green Wellie so Peter invited Fiona for a cup of coffee. "I can take the opportunity of asking some of the staff about having a gold mine on their doorstep," he told her.

As they walked through the shop Peter spied a bottle of Tyndrum "gold" whisky. Well, that must be a first, he thought to himself!

After their hot drinks they walked back through the shop and Peter stopped and spoke to a lady shop assistant. He asked her about the bottle of gold whisky.

Not realising who Peter could be, the lady replied. "We have our very own gold mine here in the village. It is deep in that mountain across the road so a local whisky distillery thought it would be a marketing opportunity to sell Tyndrum gold whisky."

"And how do people here feel about a gold mine in your village perhaps creating lots of jobs and bringing tourists," remarked Peter.

The shop lady replied that not many local jobs had been created so far and there was nothing for tourists to see as the gold mine was hidden far into the mountain range. "The Australian mining company have brought their own mining engineers with them although there are a few Scottish executives involved with the local administration, but it is so heavily guarded there is simply nothing for tourists to see. Perhaps in the future it might make a difference but to be perfectly honest it is unlikely to have any positive effect on our small community in the short term."

Peter thought it better not to pursue talk of the gold mine and thanked the lady for her time.

Fiona had listened without comment but when they were out of earshot she said to Peter. "There is some strong feeling here. It might not be such a good thing to stir up a hornet's nest!"

They got back into the Enterprise hire car and having studied a possible route back to Ardgartan set off in the direction of Crianlarich. Fiona explained that the railway from Glasgow into the western Highlands split at Crianlarich, one branch of the West Highland Line going to Oban and the other continuing over Rannoch Moor and eventually down into Fort William.

Fiona thought they would be hard-pressed timewise to take in the Loch

Achray hotel on this trip and as Peter was moving there on Tuesday it would be better to wait.

It was mid-afternoon and the road took them down the side of the top of Loch Lomond. Views were spectacular with snow still on the top of Ben Lomond. "In parts of the Highlands we can have snow on the very highest peaks the whole summer long," said Fiona.

Within the hour they were at the road junction where they turned back towards Fiona's own village and then onwards to Ardgartan. "Do you want to drop me off at home and come and pick me up later, Peter, or I could come back to your hotel now and have a quick wash and brush up in your room before dinner?" asked Fiona.

Peter said he would leave the choice to her but they could enjoy longer in each other's company if she decided to come back to his hotel. "That's settled then," said Fiona. Back to your hotel and you can tell me a little more about yourself. You have been very sparse with personal details so far Peter Kingston," she winked.

They drove in silence for a few miles before Peter said. Let's enjoy a pre-dinner drink in my room and I will try and answer any questions you want to put to me," he said. Once parked at the hotel they stopped at Reception and Peter asked if it would be OK for them both to have dinner. "Of course, Mr Kingston," said the Receptionist. Dinner will be at 7.30pm.

In the hotel room Fiona phoned home and said she would be in late. "I'm having dinner with Peter Kingston at Ardgartan." I'll either call a taxi or Peter can run me the short distance home," said Fiona.

While Peter poured a couple of gin and tonics Fiona used the large and elegantly finished bathroom for a wash and brush up. She emerged looking both refreshed and even more attractive than Peter had remembered from earlier.

Cheers! and they sat in two chairs at the bedroom window looking down Loch Long. It was just minutes before Fiona asked. "Have you recently suffered a personal disappointment, Peter? During today there have been times when I have felt you mind could have been elsewhere?"

It was time to spill the beans. I had a lovely girlfriend, and I really thought our relationship might have been going places. You read about my kidnapping and plane crash last year here in Scotland. Well, she helped me through some difficult months and once back home I got myself back into work and she at her photo-journalism job in London. But when I said I was coming back here to Scotland to write articles this week on behalf of Lochs and Glens Holidays for my newspaper she dropped the bombshell that she had been offered – and has accepted – a job in America," said Peter.

Fiona just looked at him in silence for a few minutes before saying. "That obviously hurt; hurt you very much, so where does it leave your relationship?"

Yes, very upsetting," said Peter "But she obviously feels she has a future career more important than our relationship and I will not stand in her way. So, I will pick up the pieces of my life, and well …here we are but maybe I am being presumptuous … do you have somebody in your life Fiona, asked Peter?

"I did have but we are facing similar circumstances Peter. Mine ended a few months ago and yours has only just ended. But who knows our meeting might have been meant to happen although I certainly do not want you to think I am being pushy. But in the short time I have known you I really enjoy your company, I think you have a very interesting life and I would like to spend more time with you if that is what you would also like?" said Fiona.

"I feel the same," said Peter. "Don't take this the wrong way but let's not rush things. A nice dinner this evening and perhaps we can meet later in the week? I have articles to write in the coming days for Lochs and Glens and next week I am writing travel articles based on things that are different here in Scotland for the English visitor. I feel the gold mine is just one example of the "unknowns of the Highlands". I had thought it was only whisky to be found amongst the heather and I would never have dreamed of gold!" he remarked with a smile.

They chatted more about each other's "earlier days" and there was little doubt in Peter's mind that here was a young lady that he wanted to spend more time with.

Then it was time for dinner. "Let's go downstairs and we can chat over our meal Fiona if that's OK with you?"

They sat at a window table for two and from the extensive menu, both Peter and Fiona decided on the same dishes; Carrot and Coriander soup, followed by chicken and ham pie with some cheese to follow. When it came to drinks Fiona ordered a glass of white and Peter stuck with lemonade and lime, remembering he was driving Fiona home afterwards.

Over the meal they chatted about Scotland, Fiona's upbringing in the Highlands and her hopes and aspirations for the future. "I certainly have no intention of being a career girl. It might be unfashionable, but I think I will be more suited to a domesticated homely life," she chuckled.

They had coffee in the vastness of the lounge where leather settees and huge leather chairs had been arranged in lines to allow guests to enjoy the dramatic views down Loch Long. The glow of the orange lights from the shipping and naval terminals in the far distance provided a stark contrast to the tree covered slopes of the hills which came down to meet the shoreline as far as the eye could see.

By 10pm the evening was nearly over and Peter said he would run Fiona home. You have to go to work and I have to start writing early," said Peter. "I also have to contact my Editor and let him know how things are progressing."

They drove back to Fiona's village in silence but pulling up a short distance from her home they turned to each other. No words were necessary. They looked and kissed, a warm tingling sensation running down Peter's spine. Fiona's left hand resting on Peter's shoulder but refusing to move even when they slightly pulled apart.

Peter, this has been a wonderful day and I know we have only just met but if I said I would simply love to meet again later in the week and spend more time with you how would you react?" asked Fiona.

"I think I would like that very much and I know this is a bit corny, but my mobile phone number is on this card. I know Lochs and Glens will be asking me to move on to another of its' hotel, possibly Fort William or Loch Achray in the next day or two so please do keep in touch".

Fiona slipped a piece of paper into Peter's hand. "I was hoping you might say that, Peter. This is my personal mobile number so let me know which hotel you are next visiting and, well I would love to speak tomorrow if that is not too pushy!"

They kissed again, this time Fiona seemed to give their embrace more feeling and it seemed ages before either would let go, knowing that when they did the evening was certainly at an end. Fiona got out of the car with simply a "good night, Peter, just wonderful!" – almost to herself - and she was gone.

CHAPTER

4

Although it was nearly 11pm when he got back to his room Peter decided to call Sue. Maybe she was still awake. It rang three times and then he heard Sue's voice. He told her he was sorry to phone so late, but his day had been busy.

"Sue, before you say anything, I have decided it will be best for you to pursue your career in America. I will concentrate on my writing and work back in Surrey. Maybe our paths will cross in the future but for the time being, I have decided this is goodbye," he told her.

There was a long hush from the other end and then in a cold, matter of fact voice Sue said. "Well, that's it then. Maybe it's for the best but no hard feelings," said Sue.

It was a relief but Peter thought Sue would put up more of an argument. After all his own life had suddenly changed for the better since meeting Fiona.

Peter did not want to prolong the conversation but wished Sue every success in her new venture.

"Goodbye Sue," and he put down the phone.

For a few minutes he could not believe it had ended. But his mind cleared, his whole body felt relaxed and perhaps a new future beckoned for him too.

Peter slept soundly and dreams had been memorable. But now it was Monday morning and lots to do. Before his 8am breakfast Peter rang to his office to report progress.

"Hello Peter. Your first article on Lochs and Glens, but copied to them also, should be on my desk by tomorrow morning Peter if it is to make this week's edition," said his Editor. "I know you will be visiting some of their other hotels and some of the places guests go out on daily tours but just paint a scene with your first 1,000 word article and mention a few specifics with hotel and food descriptions but your second piece can be more enlightening on tours and why people from the south travel all the way to the western Highlands," said Bert Maynard.

Peter went downstairs to breakfast and ordered some pure orange, Scottish porridge and a kipper with toast and marmalade and a pot of tea. Just as he was finishing his mobile phone rang and it was the Lochs and Glens lady. Peter quickly left the table and went out to the main Reception area so as not to disturb – or be overheard – by other guests.

"Good morning, Peter Kingston," said Alison. "I hope you have been suitably impressed by our Ardgartan flagship hotel and you managed to have an interesting day yesterday?"

Peter assured her he had been more than suitably impressed and outlined his tour round to Inveraray Castle and also the Tyndrum gold mine village. He told Alison he would be spending the day writing the first Advertorial article which his Editor needed by the morning. "Of course I will copy you in on it and hopefully it will receive your blessing. But if you have any comments or require any changes please let me know first thing so that I can pass them on to ensure the article and photos make this week's edition," said Peter.

Alison assured him she would and would also email the newspaper directly with a selection of photos which Lochs and Glens used in their brochure.

"Also Peter, I would like you to move to another of our hotels tomorrow – Loch Achray which is over near Callander and about a one hour journey from Ardgartan. I will phone the Ardgartan Reception to give you directions but if you have a road map it is easy to find or you could put in the hotel postcode to your car sat/nav."

Peter thanked Alison and said he would hope to get his article to her email before the end of the afternoon. And with that the conversation ended and Peter returned to his room. The sun was gleaming down on the still waters of Loch Long and the reflections of the fir trees added a tinge of darkness to the still waters; still except for ripples from the fish rising to catch flies straying too close to the water!

Before settling down to writing his article Peter rang Fiona's mobile. It was answered almost immediately. "Hi Peter, oh this is so wonderful to hear from you this early. I could not help thinking of our lovely day together yesterday. What are you up to now?" she asked.

Peter said he was about to start writing having spoken both to his Editor and to Lochs and Glens.

"I will be moving hotels tomorrow over to Loch Achray which I am told is about a one-hour drive. I will be staying there two nights and then moving to Fort William on Friday. Do you know what your plans are this week?"

Fiona was nearly bursting with enthusiasm. "I spoke to our Manager here first thing this morning and I have a week's holiday owing which I could spend with you from this Friday if you would like to?"

"Would I like? I would like that very much Fiona but are you sure you do not want to spend some time at home?"

"No, I am sure Peter if you are sure you want my company. After all you will be busy touring around and writing but I will promise to keep out of your way when required," and he could feel her warm smile and glow down the phone.

It was settled. Peter promised to contact her from the Loch Achray hotel the day after tomorrow and together they could plan places of interest the Lochs and Glens guests were taken to on daily excursions.

It took Peter a few minutes to get his writing mind into gear. How could he have been so lucky to find such a beautiful lady with a warm and outgoing personality so quickly after "His Sue" had decided to head off to The States and agreeing to end their relationship?

Unlike a typical newspaper article Peter realised he had to discipline his thoughts to writing about Lochs and Glens as the Company would like it presented to readers. It was not difficult as everything Peter had heard, seen and witnessed so far had presented a very high and favourable image. From hotels to food, to coach itineraries and scenery; no wonder people from the south were being wooed to the western Highlands.

There was Inveraray Castle which has really impressed Peter, not just because he had met a real live Duke for the first time but such a nice, down to earth gentleman who sincerely welcomed visitors and was in no way "snobbish". There were the fantastic views of mountains and lochs and especially the nighttime scenes from the Ardgartan hotel to the oil and naval terminals in the distance down Loch Long.

It took Peter most of the day to polish his 1,000-word article to his satisfaction. Peter had built a reputation on taking pride and care in everything he wrote. Once totally happy and having saved to "file" he sent an email to Alison attaching a copy of the article and asking for her views and any corrections.

By 5pm and having taken a stroll around the paths through woodlands surrounding his hotel Peter found a reply waiting for him from Alison. There were two slight corrections but a request for him to phone before 6pm.

He dialled from his mobile phone and asked to be put through. Within seconds Alison was on the other end. "Hello Peter. Thank you for the article and I was really impressed. You have presented our Company in a way which I am sure will attract many people from down south. When you write your second article can I ask you to stress how we operate 12 months of the year and adjust our daily coach tour programmes to match? Also that we have "mountains and mistletoe" holidays in the run up to Christmas so if guests want to enjoy an early Christmas then we serve turkey, Christmas pudding and even Father Christmas from early December at all of our hotels," said Alison.

Peter promised to include that in his second article which would include the Loch Achray and Fort William hotels as well as a tour on Loch Ness and to the Isle of Skye." I am looking forward to the cruise with your husband, Fred, on Loch Lomond, before continuing my road journey to Loch Achray," said Peter. Alison said she would speak to her husband and make the arrangements. "He will phone Reception and let you know what time to meet him," said Alison.

Once he had incorporated the changes requested by Alison he sent a copy by email to his Editor and then decided on a long soak in a nice hot bath before the coaches returned with guests.

CHAPTER

5

Peter's Editor, Bert Maynard, phoned him early the following morning to say the advertorial article was fine and it would be accompanied across a two-page spread by 4 photos; a Lochs and Glens coach; the Ardgartan hotel; Glencoe and a Golden Eagle flying near the Isle of Mull.

Peter explained he was moving hotels; today and tomorrow at Loch Achray and on Friday he would move to The Highland Hotel at Fort William.

"Do not forget to keep in contact every day, Peter, so that we know you are safe!" Peter detected a note of amusing sarcasm. "And let me know what travel articles you have planned for next week once the second and last advertorial has been filed," said his editor.

Peter assured him he would but before the call ended Bert Maynard broke some additional news to Peter.

"There have been two further jewellery shop raids in the south and in both instances the thieves just concentrated on gold items. The police are baffled and have no leads but it may have something to do with the price of gold on the world market has now risen to just over £1,000 an ounce. But that's for the pure stuff so they may be stealing and having it melted down somewhere," said Bert. "The police have been unable to make any strong links between each of the robberies and CCTV does not show any vehicles in the vicinity of each robbery carrying the same number plates. Either the gang are using a vehicle, then dumping it and switching cars or there is an extensive network of thieves all wanting gold!"

After breakfast and having finished packing his case and laptop Peter went down to Reception both to check out and to confirm directions to Loch Achray. He also decided to phone Inveraray Castle to see when the Duke of Argyll might be able to spare half an hour for a further chat. Peter got through to the Duke's secretary in the Estate office and she asked what his programme was for the day.

"I am moving to the Lochs and Glens hotel at Loch Achray today but I can make myself available anytime during the coming three days," said Peter.

She asked if he could make 10.30 am on Thursday and he said he most certainly could. That settled, Peter said goodbye to various staff he could find at Ardgartan, put his bags into the Enterprise rental car and drove off in the direction of Tarbet. Fred had given Reception the time of 10am and the car park at the village road junction where the A82/A83 road forked to head off up the side of Loch Lomond to Crianlarich.

As Peter got out of his car, he could see Fred walking from a jetty to meet him. "Morning Peter. Sorry the weather is not better but this "Scotch Mist" should lift in the next hour. But I think visibility is good enough for you to see most things."

Having boarded the boat with Loch Lomond Cruises painted along its side, they set off with Peter having been invited up to the wheelhouse. Fred explained that some of his boats ran a taxi service across to the Lochs and

Glens hotel at Inversnaid. "This secluded hotel was once a hunting lodge for the Duke of Montrose and is steeped in local history, from clan warfare to the clearances. Inversnaid also offers spectacular views of Arklet Falls, the muse of Wordsworth and Sir Walter Scott," said Fred.

He explained that guests were transported across Loch Lomond every morning and evening to enjoy their daily coach excursions. "On the day of arrival guests are dropped directly at the hotel by the coaches and the same happens on the morning of departure. But daily during their stay it is easier for the buses to be on this side of the Loch," he said. "Queen Victoria once stayed here at the Inversnaid hotel. "She had arrived overland by Royal coach pulled by 4 horses."

Peter was shown a cave where it was reputed that Rob Roy had hidden from British soldiers. He also heard how Loch Lomond was reputed to be the longest of the lochs in Scotland although this was strongly contested by Loch Awe!

The boat journey had lasted an hour before Fred headed his cruiser back to the car park. Peter said he had been impressed and grateful for the trip and interesting information and said goodbye to Fred.

Peter got into his car and headed up the side of Loch Lomond on a single carriageway, twisting road which kept to the shoreline of Loch Lomond.

At Crianlarich Peter stopped for a cup of tea and realised he was only half an hour away from the gold mine village of Tyndrum. He strolled up to the railway station where the West Highland Line from Glasgow divided, one line heading to Oban and the other to Fort William. But speaking with station staff he learned that both lines passed on other side of Tyndrum and each had its own railway station before continuing over and round mountains towards the Scottish west coast.

"There must be a separate travel article worth writing on how the West

Highland Line was built, for what purpose and for how much," Peter said to himself as he walked back to his car. It was already 1pm so Peter headed east towards the small town of Callander. It was a journey of just over an hour and as he approached the town, he recognised the T-junction he had been told to watch out for and a sign indicating the Rob Roy Pass where the Loch Achray was located near its base.

It was a further 15 miles driving through a very picturesque valley with an expanse of water to his left and a small hydro-electric dam. He knew from having earlier studied a map that the stretch of water was certainly not Loch Achray.

He rounded a bend to see a large castle-like building, a converted stately mansion now individual up-market apartments. "Very nice too", Peter thought to himself! Round two more quite sharp bends and the road opened out with a stretch of water again to his left. A sign in front indicated boat trips on the Sir Walter Scott – "worth investigating" said Peter out loud.

There in front was a sign, Loch Achray Lochs and Glens hotel off to the right. In front of him a two-story creamy white elongated building where the driveway swept in a circle outside the front door. He parked and went in, leaving for the time being his case and laptop in the car. At Reception he introduced himself and the young lady, this time speaking with a Scottish accent and wearing a badge indicating her name was Susan – whoops, not good for memories being awakened thought Peter!

Ah Yes, Mr. Kingston. We have been expecting you. I will just call our Manager. Within a few minutes a lady appeared from a back office and introduced herself as Megan.

"Welcome to Loch Achray, Mr. Kingston. Alison has given me details of the articles you are writing for Lochs and Glens so we hope your two-day stay here at our hotel will prove comfortable. We are one of the older of the hotels within the Group and certainly different from where you have been staying at Ardgartan. However, I think you will find the same high standard of staff service, food and comfortable rooms, be they a little smaller," said Megan.

She invited Peter to see his room, first floor at the far end of the corridor. Large enough with a very nice ensuite, thought Peter. Megan explained to Peter that many of the guests enjoyed evening entertainment after dinner and at Loch Achray this ranged from Highland dancing with performances by the group from Callander to accordion and guitar. Music ends at 11pm but if you need to go to bed earlier, then this room is one of the quieter ones," she explained.

Megan said dinner would be at 7pm and back downstairs she showed Peter where he could park his car. "You can bring your suitcase in and leave it by Reception first Mr. Kingston," she explained.

He left his suitcase and laptop case by Reception and they were promptly carried to his room. Having carefully unpacked and set up his laptop Peter made himself a cup of tea as everything including a packet of biscuits had been laid out on a tray.

Peter then phoned Fiona but her mobile went to voicemail so he left her a message saying he had arrived at the Loch Achray hotel. Having enjoyed his cup of tea he then ran himself a bath and soaked for half an hour. He was still dripping wet when his own mobile rang. With a towel wrapped around his waist Peter answered. It was Fiona. "Hello Peter. Sorry I missed your call, but I was handing over a car to a client. How was your boat ride on Loch Lomond this morning?" enquired Fiona.

Peter said he had enjoyed it very much and it would add colour to his next article. He had also arranged to see the Duke of Argyll on Thursday morning and afterwards might then drive back to Loch Achray via Tyndrum and see what further information he could gather about the gold mine.

"I also stopped off at Crianlarich this morning for a cup of tea and had not realised the railway line which divided there had both lines running on both sides of Tyndrum. That must be fairly unique in the Highlands," he said.

Fiona said railways in the Highlands were fairly unusual anyway. "Some lines were closed many years ago when general cutbacks were being made and because of the terrain it was always difficult to construct a railway where you needed it to go. Did you know Peter that to get to Inverness by train from either Oban or Fort William you first go to Glasgow which is three and a half hours, then to Edinburgh where you change again and then take a train up through Aviemore to Inverness? It takes a whole day and only two hours by road from Oban?" she chuckled.

Peter said he had been reading up and when he got to Fort William one of the "musts" was to enjoy a trip on the steam train to Mallaig. "I have learned this train was used in the Harry Potter film. That should be a real crowd-puller in my article," said Peter.

Fiona said she had heard about the train but had never been on it. "I was in Fort William during the winter but the steam train only runs through the late spring to late autumn," she said.

"It's about time you took a ride. I'll book us a couple of tickets," said Peter.

Fiona had to rush off "work calls" was her parting shot and Peter decided on a shave, shower and some research reading before dinner.

He heard the first of the three Lochs and Glens coaches arriving at the hotel late afternoon. "I must find out where these people have come from," he remarked to himself.

He came down to dinner and was met at the restaurant door by the head waiter, David, who showed him to a table in the main part of the room. Peter noticed it was carefully divided into three areas and when he asked David the reply was; "It helps our staff to deal with coach passenger groups individually. If it was a free-for-all, we would have people complaining they were having to wait longer than others, said David.

Peter selected a starter from a choice of four; Pate seemed a good idea and soon there was someone taking his order for a drink. "A nice cold lager please", he requested.

For his main course Peter selected salmon with new potatoes and green beans. It was delicious and plentiful and there was hardly room for dessert. But Peter pushed himself and ordered Pear Helene.

After dinner he went to the lounge bar and saw a musician setting up and electronic keyboard. That could be a nice way of relaxing, he thought to himself.

Other guests drifted from the dining room and sat at tables with either a tea or coffee. A group of four sat on the table next to him and Peter introduced himself as a self-drive guest staying for a couple of days but thought it wise not to reveal the purpose of his visit.

"Where have you all travelled from?" he enquired. North Kent mainly around the Medway towns but one or two on our coach live on the Isle of Grain," volunteered one of them.

"I come from Surrey, Reigate to be precise, so we are not too far apart," said Peter. "Is this your first Lochs and Glens holiday?"

One of the ladies quickly said. "Good gracious no. We come twice a year, sometimes here, sometimes to Loch Awe and once to Loch Tummel which is a bit further north," she said. "It is such good value, the tours are different every time and the scenery also different depending on which hotel you are staying at."

Peter said he had spent a little time at the Loch Awe hotel and a few days ago had had two wonderful days at the Ardgartan hotel.

"Oh, that's the new one and is next on our list," said the same lady. Peter told her the views were remarkable down Loch Long and because it was new and much larger, it was different from where they were now.

"We are going there for a brief lunch visit tomorrow. I think we get soup and a sandwich but to be perfectly honest that is more than enough midday with all the food you get for dinner."

Peter agreed and asked if they had been to Inveraray Castle." That's also on tomorrow's itinerary. There is supposed to be a whisky shop in the village and we might be offered a free tasting," said the same lady.

"I can highly recommend it – and the Castle," said Peter. "I was there the other day and I was pleased it was on my itinerary."

With that he excused himself and went out to the bar. A nightcap of a small brandy might be appropriate, he thought. The music started and peering through the door to the lounge Peter noticed the musician also had an accordion. "He provides a variety of music including some Scottish ballads and encourages guests to get up and dance. He is very popular," said the barman.

Peter was going to have his brandy until the barman suggested something from the wide choice of malts might be appealing. "I don't know too much about whisky – yet," said Peter. "But I am always prepared to learn."

The barman suggested Oban 12-year-old. "It only needs half a teaspoon of water to bring out the full flavour. I can really recommend it," he said.

Peter found it quite palatable and thought he would put "Whisky" on his list of features. The different distilleries and why whisky tasted so different from one area to another.

As he was finishing the barman said west coast whiskies, especially from the "Islands" tended to be peaty and not to everyone's' liking. "I will certainly bear that in mind," and with that Peter went off to bed.

Early the next morning his mobile rang. It was his Editor, Bert Maynard.

"I hope I have not got you out of bed or disturbed your dreams," said Bert with an obvious chuckle.

"I know you have still got your second Lochs and Glens advertorial to write this week but I want you to keep your ear to the ground about any gold jewellery thefts in Scotland. There have been three more raids on jewellery shops in the Midlands and north of England and close to a £million in value has been taken. At this stage the police have no idea who is behind the thefts but a pattern is beginning to emerge and Scotland Yard officers have now been called in," he said.

The police believe they are dealing with an international gang of gold thieves who may be trying to get the gold out of the country but so far they have no clues as to how they may be achieving this. If you hear anything while you are up in the Highlands let me know immediately, said Bert. However, and I do not want to repeat this Peter. Do not get involved in anything to do with gold! You are in Scotland to do a specific job and that only.

"Gold". Peter thought of the Tyndrum gold mine but dismissed the idea of it being raided as outrageous. There was bound to be incredibly tight security and in any case there was no suggestion that gold ingots were stored there!

Peter told his Editor he entirely understood and had already formulated some ideas for his second Lochs and Glens article.

With that the call ended and Peter sat down to absorb some of the history of the Loch Achray hotel from the early days of motoring, the building of various extensions to the hotel and how the railway from Stirling to

Callander had bought tourists and prosperity to the area.

Peter's mind returned to the subject of gold of the gold thefts. It was ridiculous to think there was a connection to the Tyndrum gold mine but it would make an interesting separate article nevertheless.

"OK, thought Peter. So there have been no reports of any jewellery shop raids in Edinburgh, Glasgow, Perth or Stirling but I will be worth making some enquiries before setting out on my Lochs and Glens itinerary later and also making contact with the gold mine's owners to see if we could meet up and even, perhaps, get a visit to the gold mine itself.

Peter took his shower, dressed and went down to breakfast.

Before going into breakfast Peter asked the Receptionist if she had any information on the Tyndrum gold mine. Her face said it all. A blank. However, she gave him the address of the tourist office at Callander and also the name of someone who she said was a friend who might be able to help.

Peter went into the dining room and, to his surprise, the group was a different one to the one he had seen at dinner the previous evening so he thought he would ask at Reception where this and the remaining group had travelled from. He could also get pointers for his day's itinerary.

The receptionist informed Peter the breakfast group had travelled from Norfolk; the final group had been delayed but would be arriving soon.

Asking what attractions the groups saw during their stay, Peter was told the town of Stirling with its Castle and "old town" obviously the nearby town of Callander and the picturesque village of Killin.

"There are spectacular waterfalls and from there you could drive to Crieff where there is a crystal glass factory as well as a whisky distillery," she said.

Peter thought that would all make a very interesting day's tour and he returned to his bedroom to arm himself with his notebook and camera.

Looking out of the window he saw a coach arriving but this was not a

Lochs and Glens coach. It was European and had distinctive number plates. Unusual, thought Peter!

As the first of the passengers began to alight from the bus Peter asked the receptionist where it had come from because he thought it had foreign registration plates. To his surprise the Receptionist told Peter that Lochs and Glens had entered into a contract with a Dutch travel firm for one coach each week but only to the Loch Achray hotel. "I think it is a bit of an experiment," she remarked. "So far our Dutch friends have fitted in very well although they do like a drink in the evenings and are certainly the life and sole of the party" she chuckled.

Peter was told the Dutch group had their own itinerary each day but had to fit in with the meal times allocated to each group. "They use the ferry route from Hook of Holland to Harwich and can normally do the journey to Scotland in about eight hours using two drivers, said the Receptionist. "There was a problem with the coach last night so that is why they are late in arriving."

His attention switched from the Dutch group to the more pressing matter of his next article and to the jewellery raids throughout England. He returned to his room and put on the television news. He was just in time for the BBC Scotland Reports bulletin but there was no mention of any jewellery shop raids. So perhaps the thieves were simply concentrating on raiding jewellery shops south of the Border!

The weather outside was not brilliant so Peter decided it would be a good idea to start his second article emphasizing the different itineraries available from each hotel and how Ardgartan as the newly built flagship hotel of the Company differed from the much older Loch Achray hotel but how the high standards and cleanliness and menu were maintained whichever hotel people stayed at.

Peter thought he would leave out any reference to a gold mine from his advertorial but to keep this in mind for a separate travel article. Perhaps his Editor would be intrigued with the thought of gold bullion north of the Border!

Peter took a break and phoned Fiona. He got through on her personal number first time and was greeted by a warm "Hi Peter" reply. She said she was looking forward to joining him on Friday when he would be moving to the Fort William hotel. They agreed he should drive down from the Loch Achray hotel and meet her at her home before they both journeyed north and over the famous Rannoch Moor route.

Back in his room Peter telephoned Alison and said research for the next Lochs and Glens advertorial was going well and he would have a draft ready by the next day. She replied she was looking forward to reading it.

Next, Peter phoned Inveraray Castle and spoke to the Duke's private secretary to confirm arrangements for his visit. "His Grace will be able to spare you about an hour. Will that be long enough Mr. Kingston?"

Peter assured her it would be and they agreed a time of 10.00.

The chambermaid arrived to tidy Peter's room so he made his way downstairs for a cup of tea in the lounge. Sitting in one corner were the two drivers from the Dutch coach together with what appeared to be the lady courier. Peter introduced himself and said he was sorry they had experienced problems with the coach on the journey.

One of the drivers simply replied "thanks" and made it obvious they did not want to get into a longer conversation!

Peter found himself another table some distance away and had just sat down when his tray of tea arrived. He was still absorbing the abruptness of the Dutch drivers when his mobile rang. It was Fiona. "Hi. I have made arrangements for my visit to the Duke of Argyll and plan to draft my second article today as my Editor wants it tomorrow," Peter told Fiona.

"Well, I will get off the phone and leave you to your work Peter. But I am really excited about seeing you on Friday. We will have lots of fun during the next week," she said and with that that phone clicked dead.

Next Peter phoned the local tourist office and after a short time he was given the phone number for the gold mine company at Tyndrum. He rang the number and his call was quickly answered by a lady who introduced herself as "Pam".

Peter explained he was a journalist and was doing several articles for the Lochs and Glens Company but also and additionally some interesting and unusual articles for his newspaper back in Surrey.

Would it be possible to call in one day next week for a discussion on how gold was discovered and how much Scottish gold is thought to be in the mountains? asked Peter. There was a brief silence and Pam said she would have to speak with the chief executive of the company, recently renamed Scotgold. "Give me your mobile phone number and I will get back to you in the coming days," said Pam.

Peter thanked her and explained that on Friday he would be moving from Loch Achray to the Group's hotel at Fort William.

"That is fine, Mr. Kingston. I will see if I can arrange a meeting". Pam hung up.

Peter went out to Reception and asked the young lady if she could get the Fort William hotel on the phone. He waited and after a short time she told him to lift the receiver at the end of the desk.

"Hello," said Peter. He introduced himself and said he was expected at the hotel on Friday afternoon.

"Would it be possible to call in tomorrow around lunchtime for a quick chat with your Manager as I will be in the area and I need some information for the article I am writing on behalf of Lochs and Glens management."

The young lady at the other end asked him to hold and a few minutes later a male voice was on the phone.

"Hello Mr. Kingston. My name is Alistair MacDonald, I am the Manager of the Highland Hotel, and we are expecting you Friday afternoon. How can I help?"

Peter explained about the series of articles Lochs and Glens had asked him to write but he needed some facts and local colour about Fort William and the Highland hotel for the next article. "I can be with you about 12.30 if that is convenient?"

Mr. MacDonald said he would make time but tomorrow lunchtime will be quite busy as we have a Dutch group coming in for soup and sandwiches as part of their tour. "I believe they are staying at the Loch Achray hotel where you are," Mr. Kingston. Peter said he had seen them briefly as their arrival had been delayed by problems with the bus.

"Well I hope it is working good enough tomorrow," said Mr. MacDonald, with a hint of Scottish humour. "But, yes, I will be pleased to meet you. Just ask for me at Reception when you arrive."

Peter thanked him and said "Until tomorrow then".

Back in his room he started to write the Lochs and Glens draft article. But "gold": he could just not get it out of his mind. Why only jewellery shops in England and where were all the gold rings, bracelets, necklaces and other expensive items of jewellery going?

The various itineraries for coach trips for all the different hotels fascinated Peter. He could understand why Loch Awe and perhaps The Highland hotel might include the Isle of Mull for a day trip but surely Loch Achray and the Ardgartan hotels were a long way from a day trip to Edinburgh. Perhaps he would ask Alistair MacDonald tomorrow rather than bothering Alison again.

He also needed to formulate his questions to the Duke of Argyll for their meeting in the morning. Peter had in mind a separate article based not just on the obvious tourist aspect of the Castle and how it made money but on the history of the Dukes of Argyll. Was there a vast estate providing employment to scores of Highland people? It was a fascinating story in the making.

It was lunchtime so Peter thought he might investigate if a bowl of soup and a sandwich might be available. At Reception he was told two coaches from Loch Awe were expected in the next half an hour so, yes, soup and sandwiches were available for them so Peter so could join them.

He noticed the Dutch coach had left. The Receptionist told him they had gone out for the day after a quick breakfast. All suitcases had been taken to their rooms.

Peter asked if they had different drivers for each trip. "No, we see the same drivers about twice a month. They drive the coach back to Harwich, sometimes going back to Holland, and sometimes they have a break, down in Essex they believed. Most of the passengers are full of fun and enjoy the hills and mountains of the Highlands. After all most of Holland – they refer to their country as The Netherlands – is only a few feet above sea level. So high peaks, sometimes capped with snow, is a fascination to them," she told Peter.

With little else to do for the next couple of hours Peter took a drive from the hotel through Callander and to one of the largest antique centres in Scotland. With over 150 individual stalls and dealers under one roof, he was fascinated by the assortment of antique furniture, books and clothing as well as jewellery. Having asked for and been introduced to the Manager, Peter explained who he was and what he was doing in The Highlands.

"I am always on the lookout for the unusual which will make a travel article separate to the main Lochs and Glens articles I have been asked to write," explained Peter. He then outlined the jewellery raids which had been taking place throughout England.

"Ah, yes," said the Manager. "We have received a message from Police Scotland warning us to be on our guard. We have excellent security here both inside and outside the buildings and so far no problems. The police did explain that the jewellery raids down south had only involved gold items so as a precaution those dealers with cabinets filled with nothing but gold items have been recommended to fit extra security measures which I am sure you understand I do not want to go into detail about."

Oh, quite so", remarked Peter. "But I am curious why just gold. Any thoughts yourself?"

The Manager explained that whilst markets around the world did often fluctuate, gold was probably the most stable form of currency. This is why the Bank of England and Fort Knox in the USA – to name but two – hold vast quantities of the yellow metal. "By the way, did you know we have our own gold mine in Scotland now," he asked Peter.

"Yes, it is on my itinerary and I have already contacted Scotgold to ask for a visit."

He was invited to wander around and then, after a cup of tea in the adjoining café, Peter made his way back to Loch Achray and a shower before dinner.

He had time to write more of his advertorial, taking the opportunity to highlight the difference in the scenery in The Trossochs where Loch Achray was located, compared to other areas of The Highlands. He remembered Alison's request to mention the Christmas season and the slightly different itineraries.

Once he had visited Fort William he could add something of the history of that hotel as well as attractions on the west coast. He had also highlighted the fleet of coaches used by the Company. He had already peered inside one and had been impressed by the standard of comfort and the amount of leg room. Each coach had a toilet: important for groups although Alison had told him whatever the length of journey the coaches stopped every two and a half or maximum three hours.

The route over the famous Rannoch Moor was well worth a mention as Peter had already researched it and discovered it was once covered by an enormous depth of ice and snow and in present day terms was viewed as the largest area of boggy moorland in Europe covering about 50 square miles. Not a place to wander off marked trails, thought Peter!

After a delicious dinner of Scotch broth soup, fish and then lemon meringue tart. Peter made his way back to his room and phoned Fiona. She was thrilled to hear from him.

Oh, Peter. Just one more day and I am so excited because we will have a whole week together.

Peter said he was also looking forward to their time together and then outlined his programme for the next day. "I simply must get my article finished by tomorrow afternoon so that my Editor gets it before teatime. Including something about The Highland hotel is important so that readers can understand the difference in each of the hotels and how the scenery changes from area to area."

Their call ended after about 20 minutes. He had asked how her Mother thought of her going off for a week with Peter and she said her Mother was "quite relaxed". "She knows you have so far made me happy," said Fiona.

Peter got back to his writing, read and re-read the article, identifying the places he needed to put the finishing touch to the next day after his visits to both Inveraray Castle and Fort William. After a quick wash, he curled up in bed with dreams of the forthcoming week with Fiona.

CHAPTER

6

Peter was up early and had just showered when the phone rang. It was Bert, his Editor. "How is the next advertorial coming along Peter," asked Bert. Peter assured him he would have it by the end of the day. Peter thought it best to steer clear of any reference to the gold mine at this stage.

Bert said he looked forward to hearing from Peter at the end of the afternoon and that ended the call. Next, Peter headed for breakfast and left the hotel just after nine. His policy had always been to be ten minutes early rather than five minutes late!

Arriving at Inveraray Castle car park Peter was surprised he was shown to a separate parking area near the entrance and then met at the Castle's front door. "His Grace, the Duke, will be with you shortly Mr. Kingston. Please wait in this private lounge for a few minutes".

A few minutes later the door opened and a smiling Duke came into the room this time dressed in his kilt and sporran. "Hello Peter. It is good to see you again. I suggest we go to my private apartments."

They left the lounge, walked across the main entrance hall and again through the door leading to the Duke and Duchess's private quarters. A tray of tea appeared with some cake. "Homemade by my wife who loves cooking when she gets the chance," chuckled the Duke.

Peter said he wanted to write a separate travel article about Inveraray Castle and the history of the Dukes of Argyll. "It must tens of thousands of pounds a year for the upkeep of this magnificent castle, do you raise enough income from the many tourists who visit or does your Estate subsidise the running costs?" asked Peter.

The Duke explained that tourist visits alone were not enough to cover the running costs. "Of course sales at our shop and café do help but the extra money needed comes from the extensive forestry felling. We have an agreement with the Scottish Forestry Commission to lease large areas of our Estate to them and areas are cleared and replanted on a 12 to 20 year cycle," he said.

Peter was fascinated to learn the current Duke – a member of the Queen's official Scottish bodyguard - was the first in the long line of Dukes of Argyll not to have chosen a military career. "I decided when I was a teenager I wanted to concentrate on economics and land management. So I spent some years away at University gaining the relevant degrees," he said.

Finally, Peter approached the subject of gold. The Duke looked at Peter and his short answer said it all. "I wish!" Peter asked if there was any possibility of the gold seams at Tyndrum extending across to the Duke's land. "Quite a few geological tests have been done in the area but so far there have been no traces of gold anywhere near here," he said, "and the cost precludes the conducting of more testing for now".

With that the hour was up and Peter thanked the Duke for his time. "Not at all, Peter. "I have really enjoyed our chat and I look forward to reading any articles that you write mentioning Inveraray. In the meantime, if you have any other questions just give my secretary a call."

Peter thanked the Duke and made his way back to his car. He studied his map and decided the best route was to head towards Oban, and then along the coast road and Loch Linnhe His sat/nav told Peter it would take just under an hour so a nice comfortable drive with an opportunity to take in the scenery without rushing to get to The Highland hotel at Fort William.

The scenery was terrific. He passed Loch Awe and the hotel of the same name where Peter had made his recovery after his plane crash. That brought back memories and immediately reminded him of Sue. Both were now "things of the past" and best forgotten.

He turned off at The Falls of Lora, six miles north of Oban, and headed over the Connel Bridge and passed Oban airport. So this is where the plane had crashed with Peter inside a large wooden box. It sent shivers down his spine. Had not the airport firemen spotted the wooden crate before flames engulfed the entire plane Peter would not have survived to live another day.

Awful and not worth a dwelling on, if possible!

He arrived at Fort William in plenty of time for his visit to The Highland hotel so he drove along the Lochside to the far end of the town where there was a distillery at a roundabout. The road straight on indicated Inverness; to the left Mallaig so Peter turned back on himself, hoping to spot the hotel which he had been told was on a hillside overlooking the Loch and town.

As he approached the town's hospital on the left and the railway station to his right he peered upwards and there was the large hotel. No mistaking the impressive structure so at the first opportunity Peter took a left turn and followed the road until an impressive driveway and sign announcing "The Highland hotel, Lochs and Glens" loomed ahead. Following the driveway he was struck by the impressive building which was quite different from any of the other three hotels he had so far visited.

He parked and approached the front door up a flight of wide, granite steps. The door opened and a tall youngish looking man said. "Peter Kingston? I am Alistair. We spoke on the phone."

They went in and sat in one of the lounges were there was a roaring log fire. Alistair explained he was expecting the coaches from Loch Achray within the next 30 minutes so now was a good time to chat. "When the coaches arrive I will be very busy," he said.

Peter began by explaining he would be accompanied by a lady friend for his week-long stay and would that be OK? Alistair smiled and said as Peter had a large ensuite bedroom it would make no difference. Peter said he would meet the cost of the lady's stay.

I am sure we can sort something out at the end of your visit," said Alistair.

So Peter started with the first of his list of questions and made notes as Alistair spoke. He was given the history of the hotel (originally known as the Station Hotel) which intrigued Peter and also its location. "You will have noticed that we are fairly unique by being located in a town unlike Loch Awe, Loch Achray, Ardgartan, Inversnaid and Loch Tummel hotels which are all quite a distance from the nearest town," said Alistair.

Peter asked about coach itineraries. "Well the Dutch set their own programme in consultation with our head office but they like to get to see some of the other hotels which vary from week to week. As with Lochs and Glens coach visitors the steam train from Fort William to Mallaig is extremely popular between spring and autumn when it is running."

Peter just had time to ask one more question before the first of the coaches appeared. "How do the Dutch fit in?" asked Peter. At first Alistair appeared taken aback by the question. Then he answered. "The guests are great and love the mountains, especially Ben Nevis as Holland is quite unlike anything we have here. However, the drivers appear quite reserved and keep themselves very much to themselves."

As Peter got up to leave the two Dutch drivers and the courier appeared. They looked very surprised to see Peter and were about to ignore him when Peter smiled in their direction and politely said. "Hello". It was returned with an unfriendly scowl.

Par for the course, thought Peter.

A large team of waiters and waitresses appeared and as the guests flowed in through the front door they were shown into an adjoining dining room. Soup and sandwiches followed, and Alistair excused himself.

"Now I must work so I look forward to seeing you again tomorrow afternoon Peter. Have a safe journey back to Loch Achray,"

As he got into his car his mobile rang and it was Pam from the Scotgold mine. "Ah, Mr. Kingston. I have managed to arrange a meeting with our chief executive, Richard, who says as you will be making your way from Loch Achray to Fort William tomorrow, he can see you at 11.00. Will that be convenient?"

Peter assured her it would be. "That is most kind". Pam gave him instructions on how to find their office on the outskirts of Tyndrum just before the start of the village. See you tomorrow, replied Peter.

His journey back took him through the awe-inspiring Glencoe. The mountain of the same name still had patches of snow on the summit and in gullies. The road had climbed after leaving the village of the same name and the mountains on both sides closed in, then it narrowed and Peter noted it had been blasted out through large boulders. There were several sharp bends and Peter wondered how a large coach and lorry could pass. On the next bend his question was answered as he had come up behind a large logging lorry and a tourist coach was coming in the opposite direction. Both slowed and with only inches to spare each safely passed. "Wow", thought Peter. I would not like to see that done in the dark!

The road levelled out, the pass widened and Peter realised he was approaching the famous Rannoch Moor. On his right he saw a sign with directions to the Glencoe Ski Centre. But he had little time to take in the scenery as an opportunity to pass the logging lorry presented itself with a straight stretch of road ahead and no traffic approaching. Once passed the lorry the road was relatively clear and Peter made good progress.

It was not long before the road descended and he was soon approaching the village of Tyndrum where his meeting the following morning would take place. No time to linger now, thought Peter as he wanted to get back his hotel and complete his Advertorial.

Once back in his room he had an hour to put the finishing touches to the article including quite a lot of what he had seen and been told during the day. Just before five he phoned Alison at the hotel head office and said he would be sending over his article by email and, at the same time, forwarding it to his Editor.

"If you have any changes or suggestions I would be grateful if you could let me have them by the end of the afternoon," said Peter. "By the way I had an interesting and informative visit to The Highland Hotel so that I could incorporate my thoughts," he told her.

Next he rang his Editor, Bert, and said the Advertorial would be emailed shortly. "For what it is worth Loch Achray has a Dutch coach party once a week and whilst the holidaymakers are a happy bunch, the two drivers and courier just act suspiciously every time they see me," Peter told Bert. "It is probably nothing but somehow, I have a gut instinct all is not what it should be. I am told it is usually the same drivers for each trip, sometimes getting a week's break, but invariably the same people. They collect the coach when it arrives from Holland at Harwich and then drive it back and hand over to another crew who take the coach and passengers back to Holland," said Peter.

Bert told him to try not to read too much into the situation. "Whilst I usually trust your gut instinct Peter, you have only just encountered these people and perhaps it is no more than a "chemistry thing!"

"Anyway, I look forward to reading the Advertorial and if Lochs and Glens want any changes, let me know by breakfast time in the morning. Your first article and photos, published today, have been very well received and quite a few readers have emailed the newspaper asking when the next Scottish article will be published," said Bert.

Having sent both a copy of his article, Peter had just settled back to relax with a cup of tea made in his room when the phone rang. It was Alison. "Hello Peter. The article is once again very good, but I would like a small change, please. Can we delete the reference to our new Dutch business? It is an experiment for one year only before we make a final decision on whether to continue with it is future years. We do not wish our more conservative UK customers to think we are going to encourage European customers. After all we have built our business over the past 30 years with a strong home base," said Alison.

Peter said it would be no problem to delete the small reference to the Dutch at Loch Achray. He emailed his Editor with an instruction to delete the sentence mentioning them.

CHAPTER

7

The following morning Peter was up early and having packed, he rang his Editor to remind him it was the day when he was moving to Fort William and The Highland hotel where he would be his base for a week.

He told Bert he would be writing separate travel articles about Inveraray Castle and the Duke of Argyll as well as the gold mine at Tyndrum.

"They have kindly arranged for me to meet at the gold mine offices this morning as it is on my route to Fort William," Peter told Bert.

"OK, Peter, but take care and even if you discover a rich seam of gold, remember you have a job here in Surrey," chuckled Bert.

After thanking the Receptionist for his stay, Peter loaded his case in the car and set off to collect Fiona from Tarbet. It was an uneventful journey of just 45 minutes and as Peter pulled up, he saw Fiona looking out of the front window. The door of the house opened, a smiling Fiona came running down the path with her small suitcase barely giving Peter time to get out and open the opposite car door for her. She was wearing black trousers, a clingy grey sweater and a green anorak with the zip unfastened.

She dropped the case by her feet, gave Peter a warm hug and kiss and said. "Let's go. I am so excited!"

As Peter got back in the car he noticed a lady, who presumably was Fiona's Mother, standing by the door. Peter smiled. Fiona waved and they slowly drove off. It was a few minutes before either of them spoke. Peter asked if that was her Mother at the front door. "Yes, and she is happy for me and already knows quite a lot about you," said Fiona. Since that first day we met I have shown her reports of what happened to you at Oban and also why you are here this time."

Peter nodded but made no comment.

Then Peter explained they would be stopping at Tyndrum as he had a meeting with the gold mine company. "That's no problem, Peter. Just to be with you for the next week is fine whatever you have to do. I know your work is very important," said Fiona.

They drove in silence for a while and then Peter turned slightly in Fiona's direction and said. "I don't know what has happened but you have suddenly made me feel very happy and contented, Fiona."

Oh Peter, I feel exactly the same but I was worried you might have thought I was being pushy. We have both suffered emotional problems recently and perhaps our meeting was meant to be. I just hoped you would feel the same way towards me?"

Peter smiled and they both knew there was chemistry at work.

The sun was shining when they arrived at Tyndrum. The office of the Scotgold Company was in a former station office building at the railway station. As they walked the last few paces a lady came out and introduced herself as Pam. "We spoke on the phone. You must be Peter Kingston." They shook hands and Peter introduced Fiona.

"Fine. Come away in. Richard is keen to meet you," said Pam.

Richard was standing in the office behind his chair. He was about 6ft in height with an excellent tan and Peter guessed about mid 40's in age. He had a rugged appearance and was obviously not someone who had sat in a cozy office and been a paper-pusher all his life.

"Hello Peter, and this is …?" Peter introduced Fiona. They were invited to take a seat and Pam asked if they would like tea or coffee. Both replied they would like coffee.

"Well, Peter, you obviously want to know about our gold mine and I suppose understand a little about gold mining in Scotland?" Peter said he wanted to write a separate travel article about the discovery of Scottish gold and obviously needed to understand how it was discovered; how much gold existed; and who was behind the mining exploration.

Pam came back with a tray of coffee and Scottish shortbread biscuits. Richard asked if Peter minded if Pam stayed to take a few notes. "When it comes to journalists and articles, it is essential I know what I might have said just in case any of our investors and board members think I might have spoken out of turn, he said with a smile.

Peter assured Richard it was not his intention to write anything controversial. "I just think from a travel and tourist point of view the discovery of gold in Scotland will prove really interesting to our readers in the south," said Peter.

Richard started by explaining the mining had been taking place in the Scottish Highlands for hundreds of years and more than a century ago there was far more interest in finding lead. "There are numerous mine workings in this part of Scotland and indeed it is as a result of one of the lead mine headings that we discovered gold," said Richard. "But you must understand there are no ingots waiting to be collected or nuggets the size of marbles sticking out of the rock for us to find. It is far more scientific than that and a lot of work is involved in just obtaining an ounce of gold. We probably mine, crush and wash several tons of rock and separate out the Pyrite which in turn contains the traces of gold. Once we have refined on site enough to produce gold ingots these are taken to the Assay Office in Edinburgh to authenticate whether they are 24; 22 or 18 carat," he explained.

Peter listened intently to how the jewellery trade could bid on the gold and how an alloy with a trace element was added to ensure it could always be identified as gold from the Scotgold mine. The jewellery trade usually like gold assayed at 18 carat as 22 carat was softer although much purer.

"Do you believe there is more gold in the area?" asked Peter. "Most certainly and we have an arrangement with the Scottish Government to license us to work other areas once we have established there is a profitable amount of the mineral to be mined," said Richard.

Peter asked if it was a case of panning for gold in local rivers or something a bit more scientific. Richard explained that whilst small deposits of gold in local streams would probably identify something more significant in local hills or mountains drilling did take place before geologists could determine the approximate area of gold.

"For example," said Richard. "Our present area of mining extends upwards like an upside down helter skelter and we are confident there are many millions of £s of gold yet to be extracted."

Peter whistled softly. "I think buying a few shares in your Company now might be a long-term good investment," he said.

Finally, Peter asked if it might be possible during the coming week to visit the mine to get "a first hand-feel of the operation to extract rock and finally gold" said Peter. "I am sure that will not be a problem but wear boots or strong shoes and old clothing. It is very dirty and a lot of dust," said Richard. Just phone Pam the day before you want a visit and she will make all the arrangements."

So he and Fiona bid their farewells and returned to the car.

"That was so interesting and thank you for taking me along Peter," she said gripping his hand tightly. "I am such a lucky girl to have found you Peter".

The car climbed up towards the top of Rannoch Moor and they pulled into a layby. Peter switched off the engine, turned to Fiona and looked into her eyes. "I think I have fallen deeply in love with you, Fiona. "Oh Peter. What can I say? I have only read this sort of thing in books and I never thought it could possibly happen in real life but, yes, I have felt the same since our first day together. Oh my love, I do not want the coming week to end and it has only just started. Hold me tight, very tight."

It was just after two when their car approached the outskirts of Fort William and Peter had already told her of his visit the previous day to The Highland hotel. They turned right and climbed the hill with the large sign of the hotel coming into view at the start of the driveway.

They carried their suitcases in through the hotel and Peter introduced himself to the Receptionist – a different lady from the previous day. Within minutes Alistair appeared. "Hello Mr. Kingston. Good to see you again and this must be?" Peter introduced Fiona.

"Your room is on the third floor overlooking Loch Linnhe with a second view from a side window looking towards Ben Nevis and I think it will suit you both. Dinner is at six thirty," said Alistair.

Taking the lift to the third floor they entered the spacious room 304, the large ensuite on the left. There was a large window which gave superb views across Loch Linnhe to hills on the far side.

Putting their cases down, they turned, looked at each other and within minutes were locked in a lingering, warm embrace. Words were not necessary. Fiona's heart beat ever faster, Peter ran his fingers through her hair and kissed her gently on the cheek and then more passionately on the lips. They sat on the end of the bed and were soon laying alongside each other.

Neither wanted to rush the moment but Fiona took Peter's hand and gently placed it on her firm breast and a special tingling ran down his spine. He turned and faced her." Oh Fiona, are you sure?

"Shush, Peter my love. Yes I am sure, it will be wonderful."

Slowly but purposely, they removed each other's clothes and, laying naked, Peter moved his hand up from her firm and fully rounded left breast to her neck and kissed her right nipple. As his tongue gently caressed the now firm and erect nipple she squealed and wrapped her legs around him. Peter has already risen to the occasion! He kissed her neck, her stomach then kissed her thigh and she pulled him over on top of her. It felt so natural, but both knew it was a special "first". There was no rush, each savouring the moment, but the climax arrived at the same time for both of them with Fiona letting out a muted squeal of delight and Peter a groan.

They lay spent still wrapped together and it was an age before either wanted to move. No words were necessary. They looked into each other's face and the expressions spelt "wonderful".

With the duvet pulled over each other they slept for an hour before Peter woke and suggested they showered before dinner. "Would you like to go first Fiona?" he asked. She suggested he went first so that she could enjoy another 15 minutes of "warm memories!"

Having shaved and showered Peter returned to the bedroom to find Fiona blissfully sleeping. He sorted out his suitcase and the casual shirt and trousers he would wear that evening before he went over and gently stroked her hair and whispered "Fiona". There was a soft "yes" response.

Sitting on the side of the bed he leaned over and said. "Fiona, its' time to shower and get ready for dinner." She opened her eyes, smiled and told Peter she had been having such a wonderful dream.

"Maybe we can share pleasurable dreams together later but right now, madam, its' time to get ready and he began to pull back the Duvet. "Peter Kingston. Don't you dare or I shall have to deal with you very severely later," she said laughing. "In that case". And with a big tug he pulled the duvet right back exposing her curvaceous body. "I am tempted to skip the meal and take the consequences!"

They laughed and rolled on the bed together before he stared into her eyes and said: "It will be much more fun to eat and wait until later when we will have the whole night to ourselves," said Peter.

Dinner comprised Leek and Potato soup followed by a generous helping of roast beef, followed by whisky sponge pudding and topped with custard. Their conversation had been in fairly general terms, each telling the other a little more about their past. Fiona explained she had been born on the outskirts of Edinburgh and had spent much of her schooldays in the City. But her father's work had brought him to the west coast on The Clyde before a freak accident had ended his life prematurely.

"Oh Fiona, I am so very sorry. It must have been very difficult for you and your mother?"

Fiona said the first couple of years had been difficult but after moving to Tarbet her mother had immersed herself in village life and had made many friends. "She is happy and settled now and also wants me to be happy," said Fiona. "When my last relationship ended some months ago, and it was little more than a close friendship Peter, she worried for a few weeks but at least I had my work at the car rental company. My Mother always said something would come along and, well, here you are," she smiled.

After dinner they took their coffee into the lounge and learned that the evening's entertainment would include a lady singer who had won international acclaim with several of her songs and lived on the outskirts of Fort William.

Although the music did not start until nine, the lounge was packed when Paula began her repertoire with a wonderful selection of Scottish and internationally known songs. Peter learned that Paula would also be singing the following Tuesday and Wednesday evenings.

Well worth making the effort to listen again, he had said to Fiona who agreed the lady had a wonderful singing voice.

Back in their room they switched on the television to watch the ten o'clock news. Second item on was a piece about yet another jewellery shop raid, this time in the Birmingham area when tens of thousands of £s worth of gold jewellery had been taken. A police superintendent said they had no immediate clues, other than it was thought it was yet another raid in a long line of jewellery shop thefts which had taken place all over England. It was believed a criminal gang with links to Europe had been involved.

Peter had slipped into his pyjama trunks whilst Fiona had produced a flowery set, comprising a button-down top and short bottom.

They snuggled together, watched the rest of the news and then the weather. "Looks as if we will have a warm, sunny day together tomorrow, Fiona. Any thoughts on what you would like to do?" She giggled and said. "Stay all day in bed!" Peter squeezed her hand, smiled and said they should enjoy the sunshine and leave bed warming until a wet day.

"Oh, what a shame," she said and ran her fingers across Peter's hairy chest.

He pulled her towards him and unbuttoned her top. Admiring her breasts he bent his head over onto her chest, placed his mouth over one of her nipples and Fiona gently groaned. "Oh Peter. Don't stop, Oh Peter."

And their love making began all over again.

When it was all over Peter was exhausted but blissfully happy. What a girl.

CHAPTER

8

After breakfast the next day they decided on a journey along Loch Linnhe and to Oban. Perhaps some fresh seafood on the quayside as Peter had read the quayside was famous for its daily supply of fresh mussels, crab, lobster and sometimes oysters. Fiona said she loved seafood but only when she knew it was really fresh.

As they drove along Peter told Fiona he had become immensely happy since their first meeting. "I know it is perhaps too soon, Fiona, but I feel I just want you around for always."

"Oh Peter. No, it is not too soon. I just feel the same and I know your work has to always come first, but I want to be around to support you in whatever you do. You also make me very happy; they do say there is such a thing as love at first sight."

Peter pulled into a layby at the side of the loch. The views were breathtaking and for some minutes they just soaked up the atmosphere. Turning to her, Peter told Fiona that he still had quite a lot of work to do in the coming week. "I have at least two more travel articles to write. One about The Duke of Argyll and the other about the gold mine and I must speak to my editor daily as he is trusting me to produce results and not to get myself into trouble like last time I was sent to do travel writing. But I am sure with you at my side I shall be as safe as houses," he smiled and winked at her.

They drove on and soon spotted signs for Oban airport and the Connell Bridge. He told Fiona that the plane had crashed there, and the firemen had pulled the burning wooden crate from the flames. I was unconscious throughout, but I am sure they must have had a fright when they opened it and found me all curled up inside. For ages I did not want to think or talk about my ordeal but somehow, now you are with me, I am wonderfully distracted. But I do still have the occasional nightmare," said Peter.

They arrived at Oban harbour and parked at the railway station. It was just a few minutes' walk to the quayside. Everything looked so picturesque with about five fishing boats moored close together. The ferry from the Isle of Mull was just arriving.

"Have you ever been to Mull?" asked Peter. "No but perhaps someday you will take me. I have read they have sea eagles which can be seen catching fish in the bay and at the far end of the island there is the town of Tobermory with the waterfront houses all painted a different colour.

Peter said they would put it on their wish list but not for today as it would probably require an early start and a ferry booking. At the stall selling seafood Fiona ordered a crab sandwich and Peter prawn. They also shared a bowl of freshly cooked mussels in a white sauce with chopped onions, each acknowledging they enjoyed the same types of food.

After eating they walked hand in hand back into the town and gazed in various shop windows until they came to a delightful tea room offering a variety of homemade cakes.

They sat and while they waited for their order of a pot of tea and one slice of plain sponge to share, Peter looked at Fiona and said. "Nothing is more important to me than my career. But since the accident and perhaps meeting you Fiona, I have come to realise there is more to life than just work. I might have been mistaken in the past for believing I could have a girlfriend who would have to come second to my career. Life is for sharing in every aspect as I have come to realise these last few days."

Fiona stared at him for a few moments and just as she was about to speak, the tray of tea and cake arrived. They waited until the waitress had put the cups, teapot and milk on the table and departed and then Fiona continued.

"Peter, my last boyfriend did not want a serious relationship and we shared nothing like I have found with you these last few days. I must be frank and tell you I want nothing better than a home, family and someone I can love forever. I have come to realise how you throw yourself completely into your work but you have a soft, gentle side as well and I know how you have been badly hurt recently. If I can help to put that right, then I would love nothing better. Let's see how the next few days go but, yes, I believe I have already made up my mind."

Beneath the table they held each other's hand for an age before the waitress returned and said. "Is everything alright? You have not touched your tea!"

Both Fiona and Peter smiled. Not a word was spoken but Fiona poured two cups of tea and Peter carefully cut the sponge in two.

They ate in silence before Peter said. "We must enjoy the coming days, but I still have two travel articles to write so once we have finished we will make our way back to Fort William and while you shower I will start on the travel article about Inveraray Castle and the Duke of Argyll."

The journey back to Fort William took forty-five minutes. Both enjoying the spectacular views of mountains, hills and Lochside forestry.

Peter glanced towards Fiona and said he had just remembered that Alison had mentioned the Harry Potter steam train from Fort William to Mallaig. "How about we try and book two tickets for tomorrow. It could be fun?"

So arriving back at Fort William they went directly to the railway station and managed to secure two first class tickets. The rest of the eight-carriage train was completely booked as it was a Sunday. The departure was at 10.30 and took about two hours. There would be a one hour stop over at Mallaig before the return journey.

Back at the hotel Peter got out his laptop and started writing. Fiona was careful not to try and distract Peter from his thoughts as she peeled off her clothes, leaving just her pants and bra on before eventually going for her shower. Peter had glanced out of one eye and the sight of this beautiful young lady scantily clad with whom he had become so utterly besotted did not escape his attention.

How could he fall so head over heels in love with someone so quickly so soon after Sue went out of his life. It was obviously meant to be.

Dinner was quite Scottish. Stovies which was shredded meat and mashed potato with a rich sauce followed by poached Salmon and an assortment of vegetables. Both Peter and Fiona shared a plate of cheese and biscuits having filled themselves up at Oban with seafood sandwiches and then the piece of cake.

They made their way to the lounge, collected a coffee on the way and the evening's entertainment notice said it would be someone singing with keyboard and guitar accompaniment. They stayed for just an hour before going up to the bedroom.

Love-making quickly followed with each of them discovering a little more about the others "likes".

Peter had realised Fiona had very little experience in the bed department and was determined to ensure he did not disappoint her. Each time they made love he caressed her body slowly and tenderly and discovered she had various ticklish points. He found one place which brought her close to reaching a climax so he had teased Fiona to the point where she pleaded for more.

Sunday arrived and it was an early breakfast as they had a train to catch. They had asked Reception the previous evening to book them a taxi to the station for nine thirty. Peter had wanted to take some photos of the steam train before settling down for the journey as it would be something else to include in his next general travel article.

As the train set off a true Scotsman in a very smart kilt, tie and jacket came through the first-class carriage with a trolley loaded down with not only tea, coffee and biscuits, but also a choice of whisky and haggis crisps. Peter asked Fiona if she would like anything. "Perhaps just a coffee. I have never been a lover of crisps although a proper haggis for dinner is always acceptable." Peter ordered two coffees and said they would perhaps have a whisky on the return journey. Before departing the Scotsman said they should look out for the Glenfinnan Viaduct. One of the largest structures of its kind in the whole of the UK and unique as it was the first where the bridge supports had been entirely cast in concrete. They would get a fine view from their carriage at the end of the train as it curved around the viaduct to Glenfinnan station.

From here the steam train climbed through a series of short tunnels and there was only the occasional glance of the fantastic mountain scenery. But then the train started to descend and first a small loch came into view and later pure white sands and the shoreline near Mallaig. In the distance they saw two islands, one which Peter said must be Skye, the other he was not sure.

They had an hour in the tiny west coast fishing port where Peter learned there was such a thriving fresh fish trade. Indeed, the line from Fort William had been specially constructed so that fish landed could be transported overnight all the way to London and be at the fresh fish markets in the UK capital early the next morning. Wow, he remarked to Fiona.

The journey back meant their carriage was now at the front directly behind the steam engine. Sitting holding hands with their backs to the loco they could see the coast disappearing in the distance as the train wound higher and higher into the mountains. Soon they were back at Glenfinnan station where the train took on water while it waited for a two-car diesel normal service train coming from Fort William.

The Scotsman with the trolley reappeared and asked if they had enjoyed their day and the train journey. "It has been really interesting and I have learned a lot," said Peter. "Did they actually use this train and the line to film some of the Harry Potter films?" he asked. "Yes, and it brought us so many tourists. Both the railway and Fort William have benefitted greatly from those wizardly films."

Back in the hotel Peter told Fiona he must get on and finish his article about Inveraray. Fiona promised she would sit quietly. "I just love the view from our bedroom window. Mountains and lochs fascinate me," she told him.

Peter finished writing just in time to have a shower and change before dinner. He asked Fiona if she would like to read what he had written while he was getting ready. "Yes, of course Peter. "To be part of what you are doing is really interesting and perhaps I can learn about you from your style of writing."

When he came from the shower she sat and looked at him, the large bath towel draped around his waist. "Peter, that is so interesting. You have brought the Castle and the Duke to life," she said.

Peter beamed. "I do try, and I just hope my editor will feel the same when he reads it."

Fiona went to get ready in the bathroom and Peter got out his notes on the gold mine. He just could not get out of his head the numerous jewellery shop raids in England when only gold was being stolen. "Gold is an international currency but whoever is behind this must have a watertight way of getting the gold out of the country," he thought, "too risky to fence so much gold in the UK with the police now on high alert."

Over dinner of smoked salmon, roast beef and whisky flavoured sponge pudding and custard washed down with Chilean Merlot, Peter and Fiona chatted about their day and what they might consider doing the following day and for the rest of the week.

"I will be speaking to my editor first thing in the morning and see if anything new has cropped up. Otherwise, we can look at the weather and take things as they come," he told her.

Later that evening Highland dancing and a group of local pipers provided some traditional Scottish music but once it was over Peter and Fiona decided to go to their room. They were like newlyweds on honeymoon, eager to be in each other's arms exploring more and more of each other.

Soon they were naked beneath the duvet and every minute they were wrapped in each other's arms was a new experience. Fiona had learned to be patient and not to excite Peter too quickly. For his part Peter knew what parts of Fiona's body to touch and excite her too so he cautiously explored and caressed those parts which just produced gentle groans and the occasional "Oh Peter!"

CHAPTER

9

It was just before eight the next morning when Peter's phone rang. It was Bert, his Editor. "Good morning, Peter. "How was your weekend?"

Peter went into some detail about the train ride on the Harry Potter steam train and other parts of the western Highlands he had been visiting, remembering carefully not to mention Fiona. "Having a quiet time alone then," remarked Bert, but there was something of a sarcastic chuckle to his voice.

Peter asked about the jewellery thefts but was told there had been no new raids. "The police nationally are baffled. There are no leads at all, no patterns to the raids, no suggestion the same people are involved. In fact, one detective told me on Friday it was though the thieves and the gold just disappeared into thin air!"

Peter told Bert he would send over the article on the Duke of Argyll and said he had become very interested in the gold mine at Tyndrum. "I think it will make a fantastic piece as not even all Scottish people realised there has been such a huge find of gold in the Highlands," said Peter. He told Bert he was hoping to be offered a visit inside the mine during the coming week.

"Ok, but take care. I am not sure this Paper insures you for gold mining exploits," and he laughed. Peter put down the phone and Fiona came over and gave him a passionate kiss. "You and your Editor get on really well," she said.

"Peter, I want to phone my mother before breakfast and let her know I am alright."

Peter said it was only natural and he would continue to get ready. He could hear Fiona in the background. "Yes Mum, he's super and great fun to be with. I am really happy."

They went down in the lift for breakfast and Peter asked if everything was ok at home. "Yes, Peter. Mum is very pleased I am spending some time away from home and enjoying myself, thanks to you. I told her you were good for me."

Peter had porridge and kippers; Fiona ordered orange juice and scrambled eggs.

They were just leaving the dining room when Peter's mobile rang. It was Pam from the gold mine.

"Good morning, Mr. Kingston. Do you have any plans for today only I can offer you a visit inside the mine if you are interested?" Peter said he most certainly was and what time did they want him there. "Would eleven be ok?", replied Pam.

"Yes, we have just finished breakfast and I presume it will be ok if I bring my lady friend along as well?"

"Certainly," said Pam. We can supply some wellington boots and a waterproof coat for each of you. Can't promise they will be an exact fit but they will keep you both dry. Be at the office at eleven and there will be a Land Rover to take you on the overland journey to the mine. I think you should allow about three hours for the visit."

Peter thanked her and filled Fiona in on the conversation.

"I have accepted for both of us and I am hoping that was ok Fiona?"

She said it was. "It's quite exciting to be such an integral part of your working as well as your holiday life," Peter.

They went back to the room to get ready as the journey over Rannoch Moor and through Glencoe would probably take about an hour.

Arriving at the gold mine office with ten minutes to spare they saw a fairly old Land Rover parked at the side. "I presume that is going to be our transport," said Peter with a chuckle. "Who cares," replied Fiona. "I'm with you and that's all that matters."

They went up the station steps and along the Tyndrum station platform to the mine office. Pam was waiting and, in the corner, stood a middle aged and rugged looking man.

Pam said they had made good time and introduced their gold mine guide. This is Alistair Mackenzie and he owns the local farmland where we have our mine. Nobody knows the area better than Mr. Mackenzie.

Peter and Fiona shook hands and told him they were looking forward to a tour of the mine. "Hmm, it's no glamorous lass," he said.

Mr. Mackenzie's accent was really broad Scottish. Peter asked him if he had been born in the area. "Aye that I was. On the farm which belonged to my parents and their parents afore them," he said.

They made their way to the Land Rover with Mr. Mackenzie telling them the boots and coats were in the back. "You'll need those right enough. It's rugged and not friendly on the feet."

CHAPTER

10

After a journey of over a mile on a newly constructed rough track which occasionally pitched Peter and Fiona around in the Land Rover, they arrived at the mine entrance. It was certainly no glamorous scene. Nothing like in the movies! There was some rock spoil; also many bags piled up presumably ready to be taken away but Peter thought he would leave the questions until later while Mr. Mackenzie was concentrating on backing up the vehicle into a tight space.

"We have the lorry coming over from The Netherlands later today to collect the huge bags containing the sludge which in turn hopefully contains small elements of gold and silver. These get processed in a huge furnace and in due course ingots come back to Scotland to be assayed in Edinburgh. Peter decided that Mr. Mackenzie was more than just a Land Rover driver and his knowledge extended to the extraction and processing of minerals.

They all went into a building where machinery was making quite a noise. They saw bags of small rock being tipped into a crushing plant and then on a conveyor and onwards into a further roller crushing plant being sprayed with water so a type of slurry containing very small pieces of rock and dust was coming from the further end.

After this it went into a wash and then on another conveyor, all the time being kept wet, and finally onto a sloping type of draining board where it was separated into three areas.

Over the noise Mr. Mackenzie explained this final process separated out the lead, silver and gold but it was still in a slurry form. "It is after this," shouted Mr. Mackenzie, "that the slurry is processed, and trace elements of gold or silver are removed. It takes many tons of rock to finally come up with an ounce of gold," he said with a smile.

Peter had noticed that only a handful of men seemed to control this process. All were wearing ear protectors as well as yellow helmets. They walked on and entered a small back room just off the main processing area. Here it was much quieter.

"How many people are employed here at any one time?" asked Peter.

Mr. Mackenzie told him that it was a 24-hour operation, seven days a week and around 28 people worked a shift. "There are those in the mine searching for profitable-looking seams after which the rock is then removed. There is one working the digger and also the vehicle drivers. It is quite complex and some of us are able to double up on the various work duties."

Peter looked across at Fiona who had been following the conversation quite intently. She smiled and remarked. "I never thought in my wildest dreams I would ever visit a gold mine, let alone be standing surrounded by gold," she said.

The kettle was on and they were asked if they would like a hot drink. "It can be wet and cold in the tunnels we will shortly be entering said Mr. Mackenzie. Peter asked for tea, Fiona coffee and a pot of sugar was indicated at the back of a somewhat grubby looking table.

"It's where the workers come for a break. They take it in turns as the machinery must be closely watched. A breakdown, especially on a conveyor belt, could cost us thousands of £s in time and lost revenue," said Mr. Mackenzie.

When they had finished their warm drinks, they left the building and headed for the mine entrance. It was nothing like Peter had expected. It was little more than a hole in the mountainside but there was a sign over the entrance "Cononish Mine". Mr. Mackenzie saw the surprised look on Peter's face and remarked. "We do not need the shore up as the rock here is solid. Further into the mine we do some remedial work after removing large areas of rock containing quartz and other deposits as it sometimes becomes more unstable," said Mr. Mackenzie.

There were electric roof lights and a draining gully running down the side. "Lots of water comes through the rock at this level but it has probably taken several hundred years to seep from the surface to this level so far underground. But it is a constant problem," he said.

There was noise ahead and a yellow flashing light. "This is where we are currently excavating. It will get very noisy and dusty from here on in," said Mr. Mackenzie. The floor became more uneven and twice Fiona would have slipped over had not Peter been holding onto her firmly. They rounded a slight bend and there was lots of activity. A mechanical shovel was loading rock into a small tipper truck. About seven men with lamps fixed to their helmets were inspecting the wall of the tunnel.

One approached Mr. Mackenzie and they spoke but as their heads were turned away from Peter he could not hear what the conversation was about. When Mr. Mackenzie returned he said they should start to walk back to the entrance as more rock was about to be blasted. "We only use a small charge as we are working in an area where the seam of quartz containing traces of gold is very near the surface," he said.

Peter asked how much further into the mountain the tunnel went.

"Oh, quite a way but the ground is very uneven and not good to walk on as not many trucks or diggers have gone over it," said Mr. Mackenzie. Peter then asked if the gold deposits were all at the same level or did they go deeper.

Mr. Mackenzie replied he was not a geologist but understood the likelihood was they went upwards rather than further down. "You see these mountains were once sea beds and as parts of the earth thrust upwards so did deposits of minerals such as tin, copper, lead and quartz," he remarked. "The Great Glen which runs from Loch Linnhe up and through the Caledonian Canal, into Loch Ness and further northwards and out into the North Sea marks a rift between the main part of Scotland and that further north which is still moving away. Only millimetres over a century but still on the move. In the same way the Alps are still on the rise," said Mr. Mackenzie. Did you know that during the Ice Age parts of Scotland where probably covered by up to a mile deep of glacier, snow and ice?"

Peter said he had read something to that effect and decided that when he was back at the hotel he would spend a little time researching a little more about the history of the Scottish mountains and their age.

They walked out of the mine into brilliant sunshine, and it took a little while for their eyes to adjust. Back in the building they swapped their waterproof mine clothing and wellington boots for their own and asked if they could use the toilet before the return journey to the mine's offices at Tyndrum.

"It's a bit basic and, well, if the lady can wait, the toilets back at the office might be better suited to her," said Mr. Mackenzie. Fiona said she would wait but Peter said he would take advantage now.

During the Land Rover bumpy ride back to Tyndrum Peter asked for a bit more information on the finding of gold.

Mr. Mackenzie told him that vast quantities of lead had been extracted over a century before from the very same mountains. "Usually, where there is lead, there is quartz and gold. Locals have been panning for gold in the streams hereabouts for hundreds of years. There are numerous lead mine tunnels scattered all over this area," he told Peter.

He explained to Peter that some of the original lead mine workings ran close to the Cononish gold mine but as far as he knew nobody had been in the tunnels for years. "I am sure there is no gold in those workings, or I would have heard about it," said Mr. Mackenzie.

Back at Tyndrum Peter waited in the office while Fiona used the facilities. He asked Pam if there were any plans to expand the mining operations.

"There are thought to be deposits of gold right across the Highlands but it costs money to carry out thorough investigations. At present we are concentrating all our efforts on the Cononish Mine and we have an arrangement with the Scottish Government to hold licenses for mining exploration in the future. They know we have the expertise," she said.

Fiona was ready and they thanked both Pam, and especially Mr. Mackenzie, for their time and trouble.

On the way back to Fort William they exchanged views on the gold mine visit.

"You know, Fiona, not only am I fascinated by what we have seen, I am even more intrigued with all that we have not seen," said Peter.

Fiona looked at him. "You are not making a lot of sense, Peter. "

Peter sat quietly for a moment as their car made its way over Rannoch Moor, and then he turned and said. "It is obvious there are gold deposits right across The Highlands. Currently there is only one working gold mine and it is costing a considerable amount of money to extract gold from the tunnels. To locate more seams of rock bearing quartz containing gold would take huge investments, perhaps on an international scale so maybe – and only maybe – the gold jewellery raids across England may be in some way linked?"

Fiona laughed. "Oh Peter. You are in fantasy land and using journalistic license to imagine a story when there really isn't one. Let's get back to the hotel and deal with the realities of life. I need an affectionate cuddle before a shower and dinner."

He smiled and their car suddenly went that bit faster.

CHAPTER

11

For Peter and Fiona their embrace and love making once back in their hotel room was as intense as before. No inhibitions: no doubting it was what they both wanted as the week together would pass very quickly.

They discussed what they might plan to do tomorrow.

Peter told Fiona he needed to conduct some research into the history and geology of Scotland. And he needed to understand the composition of the rock bearing minerals of lead, silver and gold. He also wanted a better understanding of how the Scottish Government and the Highlands and Islands Development Council had arrived at the decision to grant an Australian company the rights to extract gold.

Peter asked Fiona if she would like to visit the Isle of Skye before their week ended. "We would drive to Mallaig, take the ferry across to Skye, do a short tour of part of the Island and then drive back over the Skye Bridge and then back down the side of Loch Ness to Fort William. It would mean asking if we could have an early breakfast and a later supper, but I am sure Alistair, the Manager, would be pleased to arrange it for us," said Peter.

Fiona said she would love the adventure. "I will know more about this part of Scotland in the week than in the years of my life so far," she chuckled.

They both slept a blissful and deep sleep. It was as though they had been together for many months, not just a few days.

It was Tuesday morning and with an overcast sky with the threat of rain it was not an ideal day for touring so it was agreed that Peter would do research and Fiona would so some reading. At Reception before breakfast Peter asked if there was a local tourist office or somewhere he could get more detailed history of the Western Highlands. At that moment the Manager, Alistair, appeared and Peter explained what he was looking for.

"Yes. In the main street there is a museum which doubles up as our local tourist office and Robbie who runs the museum is a fountain of knowledge. I am sure he will be able to answer any questions to things you cannot find online," said Alistair.

So after breakfast Peter and Fiona returned to their room where Peter Googled the history of the Scottish Highlands and was pleasantry surprised to find a wealth of information ranging from early inhabitants; Land Clearance and thousands of Scottish people emigrating to America. There was a chapter on how the Americans had taken over one of the lochs as a NATO submarine base and created a new base with thousands of sailors and support staff.

Now closed and completely cleared the land had been returned to its original state although the American base at the time of the Cold War had left lasting impressions. Many local girls had married GI's and gone to live in the USA.

There had been small references to the Highlands of Scotland containing substantial quantities of minerals but mainly lead. There was little else which Peter had not already learned during the past two weeks.

Looking out of the bedroom window, it was still dry but overcast and misty, so Peter and Fiona decided to dress warmly and walk down into the town. There was a direct route down steps from just across the road from the hotel driveway.

Once into the main street they quickly realised it was a precinct with the only traffic being delivery vehicles. As they walked hand in hand glancing at the wide range of family run shops they saw the Whisky Shop. Peter turned to Fiona and said this could prove an interesting bit of hands-on history. They were greeted inside by a well-rounded Scot who Peter guessed was probably in his mid-fifties. Peter introduced himself and Fiona and the man said the shop was often frequented by Lochs and Glens coach passengers.

The range of whisky was enormous, as were some of the prices. Peter made a mental note of some prices being just over £29 while others on the top shelf were over £100. Before he has the chance to ask more, the man introduced himself as Hamish and offered Peter and Fiona a "tasting" from a well -stocked tray of tiny plastic disposable glasses half full of brown liquid, some of a lighter colour than others.

Peter asked what they were being offered. "The lighter one is a favourite called Loch Fyne. The darker whisky is a peaty variety from the western islands," he told them. Hamish's knowledge of whisky was considerable, and he told them one of the oldest distilleries was on the Isle of Mull and founded in 1798 by a local merchant, John Sinclair. But it was not until 1823 that it was granted its first official distilling license.

"Another long-established distillery is our local one down the coast at Oban," said Hamish. He told Peter this one was built in 1794 by local brothers, John and Hugh Stevenson and continued under their ownership until 1866 when it was sold. Hamish said Oban's single malt whisky was matured in American casks for 12 years which produces a flavour of lemon and oak spice. "It is a particular favourite of both Scottish and people from "down south" smiled Hamish.

He said one of the oldest Oban whiskies was released in 1969. "But, Peter, you must remember once bottled, whisky ceases to mature. By the way, did you know Fort William has a distillery at the end of the town where the road splits between going to Mallaig and Loch Ness and Inverness?"

Peter decided that the history and production of whisky would certainly make a fascinating separate travel article and asked if he could return on another day to learn more about the Scottish whiskies.

"Aye, laddie you can that. But bring a bigger notebook. There are no less than 140 registered malts!" He told them there were 120 distilleries and was an industry worth about £5.5bn employing over 11,000 people. "Just a thought to leave you with, Peter. Every second of the day about 44 bottles of malt whisky are exported to somewhere in the world," said Hamish.

Peter gasped and decided a full range of tastings might not be in order. However, he assured Hamish he was really fascinated and would be back.

Peter and Fiona left the shop and walk through the town until they saw the museum sign. "I hope you are not finding this too boring, Fiona but research is 90 per cent of a good story. Fiona assured Peter everything was an eye opener and the more she heard the more Peter brought Scotland to life.

"I am Scottish, and I have learned more in our few days together than I ever did at school," she told him. "No wonder your editor is impressed with your writing, Peter".

Entering the building there was a vast number of artifacts, paintings and literature to view but nobody seemed available to ask any questions. There was an Honesty Box by the door so perhaps this was largely an unmanned museum. They were about to leave when an elderly man appeared from a discrete door at the far end of the room and asked if he could help.

Peter explained he was looking for a potted history of the Highlands and a few minutes later the man returned with a well-thumbed book. This should contain most of the facts you are seeking. You can have it on loan for 24 hours for a small donation or purchase it for £3. Thumbing through the pages Peter decided on the purchase and thanked the man. With that they left the museum.

He told Fiona by purchasing the book he could look through it at leisure and always have it to hand if he needed to refer to a particular part of history.

"Rather than go back to our hotel, let's find a café for a coffee and plan our last two days together. The time has flown by, and I can barely think about it ending," he told her. Fiona grabbed Peter's hand even tighter, and they walked quietly down the street until they spied a really smart looking coffee shop.

Inside it was traditionally Scottish, as were the two middle aged ladies who ran it. "Two coffees and do you have some home-made cake?" asked Peter. The lady assured Peter they would not be disappointed. She returned with two unreasonably large slices of sponge cake. "Wow", remarked Fiona. The other lady returned with a tray of coffee and asked if they would like cream or milk. They both said, cream, and tucked into the cake.

Having finished the coffee and cake Peter asked Fiona what she would like to do over the next two days. "Firstly, be with you Peter. Then anything which will help your travel writing."

Peter suggested they make their way back to the hotel and consider their options. He would like to spend a couple of hours writing his next travel article so once back in their room Peter plugged in his laptop and asked Fiona to look at some of the brochures and pick a trip or activity.

Peter had already decided his next travel article would be in general terms, rather than focusing on something specific. At some stage once Fiona had returned to work after their wonderful week together Peter wanted to make more enquiries into the Gold Mine and gain a better understanding of how the Australian mining company had been attracted to the Western Highlands.

He was about halfway through his travel article when his phone rang. It was Bert, his Editor.

"Hi Peter. I hope I am not disturbing you but there have been two further jewellery shop raids, both miles apart."

He told Peter all raids were still confined to England and nothing further north than Preston in Lancashire. Peter assured him he had heard no different.

Peter told Bert of his enquiries in Scotland and that he planned to do more research into the Scottish Gold Mine. "I am not suggesting there is any link whatsoever, and the gold extracted is still in the form of sludge which is transported every week by lorry to The Netherlands.

"There is considerable security surrounding every lorry load and when the gold returns in security vans, you can imagine there is even tighter security. I cannot see a link between what happens here and the jewellery raids. But it is an interesting thought," Peter told Bert.

He told his Editor he was writing a general travel article about the Western Highlands and Bert said he would leave Peter to it. "I will email it over in the morning," said Peter as he rang off.

Peter had barely started his travel article when his mobile rang again. This time it was Alison from Lochs and Glens.

"Good afternoon, Peter. I hope you are still enjoying your time in Scotland. Your articles to accompany our advertising have been very well received and our phones keep ringing with enquiries and bookings. The owner of Lochs and Glens has asked me to express his delight at what you have so far achieved said Alison.

"How would you like to consider doing some more articles for us to accompany an advertising campaign we have planned for other parts of the south and southwest of England?"

Peter was taken aback but quickly enthused "Yes".

He asked if he could stay on at Fort William for two more days and Alison said, yes, but she would like Peter to view two more hotels. One near Pitlochry called Loch Tummel and the other on the banks of Loch Lomond called Inversnaid. "Could you check in on Saturday afternoon and depart for Loch Tummel on Monday," she asked.

"Oh yes, I remember your husband, Fred, pointing the Inversnaid hotel out as we toured Loch Lomond from his boat."

Alison said she would speak to Peter's Editor but as she knew Peter had planned a third week at the newspaper's own expense for Peter to produce various specific travel articles, there would probably not be a problem. Alison said she would get back to Peter by the end of the afternoon.

Throughout the conversation Fiona had been sitting across the other side of the bedroom gazing out of the window across Loch Linnhe and only catching snippets of the conversation.

Peter turned to her and outlined the conversation." The Loch Lomond hotel is not too far from your home but Loch Tummel is near Pitlochry which is some considerable distance away. You will be working but we can still speak daily on the phone and perhaps the following weekend if you are off work we can spend at least two days together."

Fiona said she understood and wanted their last two days to be wonderful. "We will still be together for the drive home the following day and if I can arrange with my Manager to have the following weekend off then that will be just perfect," said Fiona giving Peter a warm, longing smile.

Peter went back on his laptop and started writing. He reckoned it would take up to an hour and as he became absorbed in his work he was unaware that Fiona had made him a cup of tea. "This will keep you going, and we can perhaps have a drink in the bar before dinner," she said.

Peter re-read his article and then asked Fiona for her thoughts.

She told him that his articles always brought Scotland to life. "No wonder people down south are phoning to make bookings. I feel as though I want to be visiting the many places you are writing about, and I am here already, with you!

It was the end of the afternoon so just time for each of them to shower. Peter thought twice about sharing the shower. That would no doubt lead to either a late arrival for their meal or no meal at all. He decided to be patient until later that evening.

On the way down in the lift Peter suggested a bottle of red wine rather than a pre-dinner drink. The menu they had read earlier indicated vegetable soup, Venison and cheese and biscuits might be appropriate. Entering the dining room, two coach parties of guests were already there and a few heads turned in their direction as Peter and Fiona entered. They were shown to a familiar table and a waiter quickly appeared to ask if they would like a drink with their meal.

Peter indicated a bottle of the house red would be good. Soon, a young female waitress, who they had not seen before, came to ask if they had decided on their starter choice.

"Yes, we have," said Fiona. "We would both like the vegetable soup."

While they were waiting someone else appeared and asked what main course they would like. "Both of us will have the Venison," replied Peter. While they were waiting for the soup he gazed into her eyes and quietly said. "It seems we have been together for an age yet in little over a week we have not only become an "item", and I do not want it to end."

Fiona said she felt the same and was just about to add more when the vegetable soup arrived. They sipped the soup in silent contemplation.

The empty bowls were removed and within minutes their Venison arrived with dishes of separate potatoes, peas and carrots. There was lots of chatter from people sitting on adjoining tables and people overheard one couple talking about the steam train and another of a trip on the gondola up to the summit of Ben Nevis.

Cheese and biscuits, another half a glass of red wine and the meal was over so they went off to find a quiet corner in the lounge near a wonderful blazing log fire. Coffee was provided by two more members of staff. Peter checked on his phone the time of the ferry sailing from Mallaig to the Isle of Skye the next morning and was surprised it was at 09.45.

He told Fiona it would mean missing breakfast as the drive was at least an hour and he had not yet checked on availability. When he did, he found the ferry was full and the next sailing was mid-afternoon.

"Well, that rules that idea out. It has got to be Plan B whatever that is going to be," he chuckled.

Before Fiona had chance to say anything Peter had got up and headed to Reception. He had spied Alistair talking to some other guests. When the hotel Manager had finished, he smiled and asked Peter how he could help.

Peter explained about Skye and the ferry and asked if there was an alternative suggestion they could consider. Alistair had two suggestions. A gondola ride to the top of Ben Nevis or a drive up the side of Loch Ness, he told Peter. There is a small but attractive village about halfway along with a castle built on a bit of a headland.

"In the past, and perhaps something to do with Scotch Whisky, people have alleged sighted the Loch's monster called "Nessie". I am not suggesting you might spy the monster but the weather promises to be quite good and it might prove to be a perfect end to your week here Mr. Kingston," said Alistair.

Back by the fire Peter sat down and outlined the ideas to Fiona. She said both sounded good, but her preference was a drive up the side of Loch Ness.

It was not too long before the evenings' entertainment started. Peter had forgotten it was one of the evenings that Paula sang, and he and Fiona became absorbed in the wide range of songs, many of which the lady singer explained had originated in Skye where she came from.

It was a lovely two hours, but the time came when Peter and Fiona decided they felt really tired and went to their room. After changing into their pyjamas both lay on the bed, turned and looked at each other. Peter was the first to speak.

"I want you to know nothing is going to change when I drive you home Saturday morning Fiona. I will still be here in Scotland, in fact for a few days just across Loch Lomond from your village and always at the end of my mobile. Even when I move to Loch Tummel it will not be a million miles away and maybe you can arrange that weekend off." It was a statement and a question rolled into one.

Fiona's response was perhaps better than Peter could have expected. "Oh yes, Peter, I just want to be with you. I respect your career and simply love your writing. I have my job with the car hire company but you will always come first. I would be lovely to feel we both want to discuss the future but let us see what tomorrow and next week bring. But I already know my mind."

They embraced. One thing led to another and it was not long before they were entwined and enjoying passionate love making again.

Friday morning the phone rang early. Both were getting ready to go down to breakfast. Peter answered and it was Bert who told Peter he had spoken the previous evening to Alison from Lochs and Glens and was in full agreement with her proposal.

"Peter, please do not forget you have two more general travel articles on Scotland to write but the extra good news is the Newspaper Group want to run your articles and Lochs and Glens will be taking some advertising as well. So your readership is going to expand into the hundreds of thousands and I can see you asking for a rise in salary soon," said Bert chuckling down the phone.

The conversation over, Peter and Fiona went down to breakfast to find two of the coaches had already set off on their days' tour. The third coach, Peter discovered, was going to explore Loch Ness so maybe he and Fiona would be seeing them later.

After breakfast, Peter had a quick word with Alistair at Reception and then they went upstairs to prepare for their day out. The weather had brightened up and a cool north westerly breeze was going to peg the temperature down.

CHAPTER

12

Neither Peter nor Fiona spoke for the first ten minutes of their drive as the car made its way out of Fort William and it was not long before their spotted a sign for the gondola station at Torlundy and Peter suggested they stopped on their way back for a quick look. But certainly there would not be time for a journey to the top of Ben Nevis and back.

They headed past Spean Bridge and Fort Augustus. Fiona had picked up a tourist leaflet from the hotel Reception and told Peter there were Loch Ness cruises from this point and also a canal for boats passing between Loch Ness and the entrance to Loch Linnhe at Neptune's staircase lochs.

"Let me know when you want to stop for the loo or a cup of coffee" said Peter to Fiona, keeping one eye on the road. She told him she would probably be ok until they reached Urquhart Castle.

The scenery was breathtaking throughout the journey and both gazed in awe at both mountains and the expanse of water of Loch Ness. It stretched for miles. Just before eleven they saw the sign for the castle entrance on the right. There was little traffic and Peter had no problem swinging across the road into the Castle's driveway.

Soon they spotted the front entrance and some parking. Several spaces near the front door were free so Peter parked up. He turned to Fiona, no words were necessary, and they kissed for several minutes. When they broke free Peter told Fiona how much she had come to mean to him and how contented she made him feel. "I really do feel the same Peter," he said.

With that they got out of the car and entered the castle. At Reception Peter asked if it would be ok to have two coffees and some Scottish biscuits. He also produced his Press Card, explained they were staying at Fort William and he was writing some travel articles.

"Would it be convenient to have a few minutes of your Manager's time," he asked.

The Receptionist said she would order the coffee and said if they would like to find a spot in the lounge opposite Reception it would be brought through to them. "I will also ask the manager if he has time to speak to you," he told Peter.

A few minutes later a nicely presented tray with cups, saucers, biscuits and a pot of coffee arrived. Fiona said she would be "mum" and, as she was pouring, a youngish man in his late thirties appeared and introduced himself. He told Peter he had been Manager at the Castle for nearly three years and asked how he could help.

Peter told him about the travel articles he was writing for his newspaper group which covered Surrey and the Home Counties and wanted to include something about Loch Ness and the legend of "Nessie".

The hotel manager smiled and said so many modern scientific expeditions had been made that "Nessie" could now be truly classed as fiction. "But it is good for business, especially with the Americans and Japanese. They love the story and arrive armed with cameras by the armload. Even a few extra whiskies in the evenings at the bar do not seem to produce any new sightings," he said.

He gave Peter a hotel brochure which also contained a potted history of the building with an accompanying leaflet about Loch Ness. "I do hope the information helps and if your article does mention our hotel, let me know," he told Peter.

Peter's response was immediate. "I will do better than that. If my article includes Loch Ness and your hotel, I will have a copy of the newspaper posted to you," he promised. The Manager handed Peter one of his business cards and said he had to go. "There is always work for me to do, nothing ever runs as smoothly as I would like" and with that and a parting handshake he was gone.

The views of Loch Ness from the lounge windows were breathtaking and once they had finished their coffees, they wandered out onto the terrace where Peter took photos for his article and one of Fiona. Her smile was infectious. They were about to turn and go back into the lounge when another guest ventured out and asked if the couple would like a photo of the two of them together.

"That would be lovely," said Fiona. Peter put his arm around her shoulder, they both smiled one of those "we are deeply in love" moments and the camera shutter clicked. They both simultaneously said, "thank you" and the camera was handed back.

"Stay happy," said a deep throated voice with a strong American accent.

They went out to Reception to pay but were told the coffees were on the house.

Back at the car Peter suggested a slow drive back so they could stop and see the Ben Nevis gondola which Fiona thought was a great idea. "We have some packing to do before dinner," she told Peter.

"Please do not remind me. I am trying not to think about "goodbyes" tomorrow even if it will only be for a short time," he said.

The journey back down the side of Loch Ness, through Fort Augustus and beyond to where they turned off to the Ben Nevis and the gondola station was quiet and without incident and the conversation was as much about scenery as it was about the wildness of the Western Highlands.

"You know Peter. Without tourists and without their purchases of whisky and other local products as well as the revenue to hotels and B&B's Scotland would be quite a poor region of the UK. "Just take my firm of Enterprise. Without tourists wanting to hire more cars than we can often cater for, our business would very much depend on hiring out commercial vans to Scottish traders," she said.

Pulling up in the car park adjacent to the gondola station, Peter was taken aback by the range of greens on the trees which stretched a considerable distance in both directions and including some way up the lower slopes of the mountain.

He and Fiona walked to where the ticket office was located, and Peter pulled a leaflet from the rack. He noted the prices which were quite pricy for a single journey. He went to the window and asked if there was a reduction for a week-long ticket. The lady produced a tariff leaflet and Peter thanked her.

At the side of the base station Peter and Fiona watched as gondola after gondola came out of the building, left what appeared to be a ratchet mechanism and attached an arm to a sturdy cable and then began the ascent of the mountain. The journey was said to be about 12 minutes according to the leaflet but could be suspended in strong cross winds. Peter remarked to Fiona that he was not too sure he would want to be stuck on Ben Nevis in any storm which then closed the gondola.

"Bit of the long walk back down," he chuckled.

Peter said they needed to get back to the hotel as he had a 1500-word travel article to write before he showered and changed for dinner. Fiona said she could finish her packing and then shower while Peter was working. She also told Peter she would phone her mother as they would be heading home in the morning.

Before Peter had chance to finish his article his phone rang and it was his Editor, Bert.

"Hello Peter. I got your message about moving to Inversnaid tomorrow for two nights and then on to Loch Tummel. Any chance of another article in the next 24 hours?" asked Bert.

Peter told Bert he was about two thirds of the way through a general one encompassing Loch Ness and the Ben Nevis Mountain. "No sign of a monster but the scenery has been breathtaking. I will email it over in the next hour," he told Bert.

"By the way Peter. Despite all the warnings and publicity, there has been another jewellery shop raid. About £20,000 in gold rings, bracelets and watches have been taken from a shop in Carlisle. Once again police have studied CCTV and footage of traffic but it just does not add up. No similar cars have been seen going towards the jewellery shop or indeed seen leaving the area afterwards. Where is all this gold being taken to and no informers anywhere in the country seem to have a clue either?"

Peter put forward his own theory. "Have the various police forces got together and considered that it could be a very well-organised overseas gang," he said to Bert.

His Editor said he would ask the police superintendent of the Surrey Force.

"Why do you ask Peter," said Bert.

"It just something that has been niggling away at the back of my mind for some days now," said Peter.

"I have nothing of substance, but I have got one of my gut feelings. I turn up anything more positive you will be the first to know, I promise," said Peter.

As the call ended Fiona came from her shower. Peter told her Bert wanted his travel article within the hour. "Is that a subtle hint that any hugs and cuddles will have to wait Peter," she laughed.

"Well, I was just thinking which one I should rush to get finished!" he told her. "My immediate decision is get the writing finished and linger over cuddles with you," said Peter in a serious voice. "In that case sir, I will remain patient for the next ten minutes wrapped in nothing more than this bath towel. After that I am not sure my hands will be strong enough to hold it in place."

Peter surprised even himself at the speed of wrapping up his travel article, checking it quickly and attaching it to an email to his Editor.

"Now, what were you saying," said Peter looking at her. Fiona fell on her back onto the bed and said, "Oh Peter, what are you thinking of," and she giggled as the towel fell from her slim, damp body.

Peter lay spent. Fiona wanted to remain snuggled up but he told her that he needed to shower before dinner. "I remember you saying you wanted to phone your mother so how about you do that while I shower and get ready for dinner?"

Fiona reluctantly agreed, turned over and reached for her mobile phone from the bedside table while Peter disappeared into the bathroom. Her Mother answered after three rings of the phone and Fiona told her the week had been tremendous. "I have found out so much about this part of Scotland that I had no idea about. Peter is a lovely man, so interesting to be with and he makes me laugh all the time," Fiona told her mother.

"We are leaving after breakfast and should be with you before midday. Then Peter has to head round Loch Lomond for access by road to the Inversnaid hotel and after two days there he will travel to Loch Tummel near Pitlochry. Oh Mum, he is so lovely and kind. I want to be with him all the time so I am asking at work if I can have the following weekend off so we can spend more time together before Peter heads back south."

The other end of the phone was quiet before Fiona's Mother said. "You seem smitten. Are you positive Peter is the right person for you? After all his writing work will probably keep him so busy."

Fiona replied that she had thought things through very carefully and although she had hardly got to know Peter fully in such a short time, she knew deep down things were right.

"Has Peter said how he feels about you? Have you discussed you being in Scotland and him way down south? It is not as though he will come home from work each day and find you waiting at the door," said her mother.

"Well, you never know," said Fiona. "But Mum, it is early days and Peter has told me things to give me lots of hope. "I think we both know there is a lot to discuss but we are both thinking along the same lines. I have never met somebody as caring, thoughtful and interesting as Peter. Let me work it out Mum, please," said Fiona.

Her Mother accepted that her daughter was sensible, if optimistic, and said she would see them both tomorrow. "Perhaps you can bring Peter in for a cup of tea?" her mother suggested.

"I am sure he will love that and be pleased to meet you," said Fiona. And with that the call ended. Shortly afterwards Peter emerged from the shower and suggested they get ready for dinner.

Over their meal and glass of red wine Fiona told Peter the main part of her conversation with her mother. Peter agreed to the cup of tea. It will be nice to meet your Mother and to reassure her I do really care about you Fiona," he said.

CHAPTER

13

The next morning, having doubled checked their room for anything that should but had not been packed, they came down to Reception and for breakfast. Alistair was there and told Peter the bill had been taken care of by Lochs and Glens. "Alison Moore seems impressed with what you have written so far, and the value of the articles will bring us lots of business," said Alistair. Anytime you are coming back this way Peter, let me know. You will always be welcome."

Peter thanked him and they went into breakfast. Both decided on a healthy and light meal, so chose fruit juice and scrambled egg with salmon.

Their cases in the car and having thanked the restaurant staff who had looked after them so well, Peter started the journey out of Fort William, down the side of Loch Linnhe and soon they were climbing through Glencoe and towards Tyndrum. Peter suggested they stop for a comfort stop and to enable him to seek out answers to a couple of questions which had been nagging him all week.

Fiona said a comfort stop would be a good idea after two cups of coffee at breakfast. She asked Peter if the stop also had anything to do with gold.

"It might have. I have a nagging gut feeling that jewellery raids in England might in some remote way be connected to a Scottish gold mine." Fiona turned and smiled at him. "It sounds like you are about to write a Hollywood blockbuster, Peter" and she laughed.

Peter glanced around, smiled and said, "Many a true word spoken in jest!"

Having travelled across Rannoch Moor in poor visibility, they came down from the high, rock strewn and flooded wastes of the Moor to fir trees and green covered hillsides. In the distance Fiona spotted a herd of deer. "Oh look, Peter. "That is the first time I have seen wild deer here. Another first with you Peter," she said.

Soon the village of Tyndrum came into view just beyond the snow gates. They entered the busy car park of the Green Wellie complex and as he got out of the car, Peter was surprised to see a Dutch coach. Surely not the same one as last week which was at both Loch Achray and then The Highland hotel, asked Peter to himself.

He made no comment to Fiona, but they strolled hand in hand into the packed Green Wellie building which was divided into a shop, whisky centre and a café. Peter asked Fiona if there might be something she wanted to buy. Fiona replied that she had all that she needed whilst their time together lasted.

Peter, on the other hand, suggested it would be nice if he took her mother a small present. "My Mother would not expect anything Peter," said Fiona. However, he thought a small gift would be appropriate. "Perhaps a small token of gratitude for your Mum allowing me to whisk her daughter away for the last week," he said.

"Only the last week," said Fiona perhaps regretting she sounded a bit too pushy. Peter, however, took it in good heart and retorted. "Well, I suppose that includes next weekend as well," he said squeezing her hand tightly. She turned, gave him a longing smile, leaned across and gave him a peck on the cheek.

They searched the shelves until Peter spied something and asked Fiona if her mother drank whisky? "She has been known to enjoy the occasional tipple. Why?" said Fiona. "How about a bottle of Tyndrum Gold?" he asked. "I think a nice box of chocolates might be more acceptable," retorted Fiona, so once purchased, they went to the toilets and then back towards the café area but decided that as they were going to have a cup of tea at Fiona's Mother's house, and it was not really that long since breakfast, a drink now was not needed.

They were about to leave the building when Peter spotted a familiar face. It was one of the coach drivers from the Dutch coach he had seen at Loch Achray. The man did not notice Peter, so he and Fiona made their way out to the car.

"Anything wrong Peter," she said. "No, but I saw one of those Dutch coach drivers in there and he seems to be spending a lot of time here in the Highlands when I thought he was taking last week's coach group back to Holland. It is probably nothing so let's forget about it and head to your mother's. She will no doubt be excited to see you after a week away."

As they journeyed, first to Crianlarich and then down the northern side of Loch Lomond towards Fiona's village, Peter said. "Fiona, I want to impress upon you my feelings have not changed and are not likely to change. Everything I have said to you during our wonderful time together I have meant, and I want it to continue. It probably sounds a bit trite but sometimes things can happen quickly when chemistry is involved. You really do mean so much to me," he said.

She leaned across and making sure it was safe gave him a quick kiss on the cheek and squeezed his knee. "Oh Peter. That is so nice. You already know my feelings and you make me really very happy."

They pulled up outside Fiona's house. Peter lifted her suitcase from the car boot and as they went up the front garden path, the front door of the house opened and Fiona's Mother stood there, her face beaming a warm, welcoming smile.

"Mum, this is Peter," said Fiona.

"I am very pleased to meet you, Peter. "Fiona has told me quite a lot about you so come in and I will bring some tea and homemade scones through and you can tell me about your holiday and journey home," she said.

Fiona led Peter into a cozy, small lounge and soon her mother reappeared with a tray of tea, three cups and plates. "I will be back with the scones," she said.

Fiona told Peter her mother liked to cook. "We do not get many visitors, so it gives her a chance to demonstrate her cooking skills," said Fiona.

Her Mother returned, poured out the tea and offered Peter a scone. "I like to cook but do not get the chance very often to cook for visitors here at the house. I do some cooking for the community when we have a function in the village," she told Peter.

Fiona then started to outline all that they had seen and done during the week. "Mum, it has been such an eye opener, and I would not have seen or learned half of it without Peter. The gold mine was fascinating as were Peter's travel articles. He let me read them and they were full of facts that even I did not know about the Highlands."

She told her Mum how Peter's Editor kept in daily contact. "I think that is probably because last time they let me loose on travel writing I finished up being kidnapped, shot, thrown into a wooden box, then in a plane crash and ended up here in Scotland more than slightly bruised," said Peter. "But in a way I am so pleased that happened because without all that Lochs and Glens Holidays would never have asked if I could return and write articles to go into my newspaper with their advertising. And without all of that I would never have met your daughter,"

Fiona beamed. Her Mother looked at them both and realised something genuine was happening.

"As long as you make each other happy," said Fiona's Mother. And on cue they both said. "Very happy indeed."

Peter reminded Fiona that however much he would like to stay longer, he had to drive all the way round Loch Lomond and then to the Inversnaid hotel. "It would have been simpler to take the ferry across, but I have my suitcase and laptop in the car which I will need first thing in the morning."

He said his farewells to Fiona's Mother and said he hoped in little over a week he would be back to collect her daughter for a weekend together.

Fiona followed Peter through the front door, down the path to the car where they said their goodbyes.

"Peter, you will phone me from the hotel later and I can phone you before bedtime. I may have to work tomorrow even though it is Sunday, but I will find time to call you. I will also ask my Manager if I can have next weekend off," she said.

Peter gave her a big, lingering hug and said he also hoped she would get next weekend off. I need to talk to you about what happens after that as I will obviously have to return south and start my proper work back on the Surrey newspaper.

"I really dread thinking about that Peter, but we will have time together before that day arrives. I love you lots". Fiona gave Peter a big kiss which he returned with warmth. Throughout, Fiona's Mother had been watching from the front window and contemplated "Had the time come when she might lose her daughter?"

CHAPTER

14

Peter's drive down the side of Loch Lomond, round the south side and then through to Aberfoyle wound through a series of small hamlets before he found himself on the road heading to the hotel at Inversnaid had taken about forty-five minutes and had been without incident. It had given him time to reflect on the time he had spent with the new love of his life and what they had discussed.

In many ways Fiona had proved to be an inspiration for his writing. He loved her company and found just knowing she was either in the background or an integral part of his daily life had given him a muse which may have produced some of his best articles for a long time.

The signpost indicated another eleven miles to Inversnaid. The scenery was rugged and sparse but nevertheless breathtaking. He needed to keep his concentration as for the most part it was a single carriageway road with an occasional passing spot. And to think Lochs and Glens coaches had to use this road every week!

His mobile rang so he pulled into one of the passing spots, not that he had seen another car on the road. It was Bert, and Peter thought it strange being a Saturday afternoon. "Hello Peter. Where exactly are you now?" asked Bert.

Peter explained he was on his way to the Inversnaid hotel where he hoped to arrive in the next ten minutes. But he had pulled over and it was safe to talk.

Bert told him there had been a development and perhaps a breakthrough in the jewellery raids across England. Police forces have combined their knowledge, studied hours and hours of CCTV and believed the robberies have been carried out by a large network of Europeans located strategically throughout England. "Their nationality is unclear, and they may have been undercover for many months while they have closely studied every location where a raid has happened," said Bert.

Peter asked if it was clear how they managed to get the gold jewellery away from each location without being spotted and Bert said the police were still working on that. "They are really baffled but if they are foreigners perhaps foreign vehicles not so far considered on CCTV footage may have been involved," said Bert.

Changing the subject, he asked Peter if there was any possibility of the Lochs and Glens travel article to be on his desk the next day.

Peter assured him he would get on with it once settled into his new hotel and certainly by lunchtime. "Various newspaper editors throughout England will be working as a team this weekend pooling our resources on the jewellery raid story so I will be in the office. And if the Group editor can put your page to bed early it will release up more staff time for this national story," said Bert.

"It is one of those occasions I wish I was back at the ranch being part of real news," said Peter. But Bert told him to enjoy the coming week's relaxation and Scottish scenery. "You will be back in the deep end soon enough Peter and I am sure this is a news story which will run and run for many weeks yet," and with that Bert said his goodbye.

Peter re-started the car and within a short time was driving down a steep hill with Loch Lomond in front of him. Just across the water lived Fiona but for the time being Peter had to busy himself with other matters.

He was greeted at Reception and shown to a specious bedroom with superb views of Loch Lomond.

"Our Manager will contact you within the hour, Mr. Kingston but anything you need, either come and ask or phone down from the room," she said. Peter thanked her, unpacked his suitcase and laptop and after a visit to the bathroom and having made himself a cup of tea sat down to begin writing.

As he began writing Peter could not clear the intrigue of gold from his mind. Could robberies of the precious metal in England have anything to do with a gold mine in Scotland? It seemed a pretty remote possibility. After all it was only in the form of slurry once extracted from the rock and processing was carried out in Europe.

Peter convinced himself he was barking up the wrong tree and continued to put the finishing touches to this, the first of two additional advertorials. There was so much about the Highlands to write about and inspire visitors from south of the border to head north. This one would concentrate on the location of Inversnaid, its history and connection with Queen Victoria. The scenery around Loch Lomond was stunningly beautiful but Lochs and Glens visitors could still enjoy daily trips out to so many nearby attractions.

The Manager at Inversnaid was named Adam but when Peter met him, he spoke with a broad accent although his English was near perfect. He told Peter he knew all about his writing work on behalf of Lochs and Glens and if any help was needed about the history of the Inversnaid hotel or arrangements for visits to nearby places of interest, Peter only had to ask.

Peter said he had two questions, perhaps both linked. "Outside of traditional Lochs and Glens visitors do you ever get accommodation requests from overseas visitors and – if so – which are the most common countries for these people to come from."

Adam replied that Inversnaid was so popular with traditional guests that very few rooms were ever spare but that in recent months there had been one or two phone calls from Dutch people asking for a room "Our Loch Achray hotel has been receiving a coach party on a weekly basis and maybe word has spread throughout Holland and people are phoning and hoping to make a reservation on the off chance," said Adam. "Other than that, we are not on any tourist hotel register and as we are so far off the beaten track such phone calls are few and far between," he told Peter.

Peter thanked him and said there was nothing else he could think of for the moment. He had articles to write both today and tomorrow and some more research around the village of Tyndrum. "Is this something to do with the gold mine, Mr. Kingston?"

Peter replied "Yes" and said he had already written an article separate from his Lochs and Glens commissions. "I am fascinated by the discovery of gold and how vast the deposits are said to be," he told the Manager.

Peter decided not to go further and postulate on any possible connection with jewellery raid shops throughout England.

He was about to go for his shower when his phone rang. It was Fiona. "I hope I am not disturbing your writing Peter but I can have this coming Friday, Saturday and Sunday off so once you have finished your stay at Loch Tummel you could drive back here. I have located a small, but quite picturesque and romantic country hotel where we could spend those days together.

Peter said it was an excellent idea and would she mind making the arrangements. I can arrange an early breakfast and be with you by about 10.30 Friday morning," Peter told her.

He showered and got ready for his evening meal. The article had been emailed to Bert, but Peter was not expecting a response unless Bert did not like what he had written.

The menu was similar to the other hotels. Peter felt in the mood for seafood so selected salmon pate and fish and chips to be followed by cheese and biscuits. As he was alone a glass, rather than a bottle, of red wine would be in order and an early night.

He lay on his bed mulling over in his mind the theft of gold in jewellery shop raids in England and Scottish gold, then any possible connection with foreign criminals and how could a coach party of Dutch tourists be in any way considered as a link. Nearly impossible Peter convinced himself and fell asleep. His dreams were not of gold but of something far more precious, the new lady in his life. It was as if he had known Fiona for such a long time.

Sunday morning and Peter had arranged for breakfast at 08.00. He wanted an early start and planned to drive over the Rob Roy Pass and Brig o'Turk before joining the main road to Crianlarich and onwards to Tyndrum.

Porridge and scrambled egg with smoked salmon, some toast and a pot of tea would keep Peter going all day. The first of the three coach loads of passengers had finished their breakfast and were making their way to the front of the hotel and down to a jetty where one of the loch steamers was waiting to take them across Loch Lomond to where the coaches were parked.

Peter confirmed at Reception that he would like to have dinner at seven that evening and with that he went out to his car and drove along the single-track road to Aberfoyle where he turned off and drove over the Rob Roy

Pass, at the bottom of which was the Loch Achray hotel. As he drove past, he spotted one of the Dutch coaches, but he did not stop. For Peter it was more important to reach the main road and climb up to Crianlarich and beyond to Tyndrum.

Once at the gold mine village he parked up at The Green Wellie complex, made use of their facilities and leaving his car where he had parked it wandered off down the road. Peter was not sure what he was looking for, if anything at all. A needle in a haystack, perhaps a new way to view the familiar was a good description but still going through his mind was the possibility of a link.

He had been wandering around for about half an hour when he saw the Dutch coach drive past and then park up at The Green Wellie. It was obviously a regular stop on their itinerary, thought Peter.

He watched the Dutch tourists getting off the bus. It was only two-thirds full so perhaps The Highlands of Scotland were not as popular with people from The Netherlands after all!

As it was a Sunday there would be nobody at the Cononish mine office so little point in wandering up there. But he was nevertheless interested in the two railway lines at Tyndrum, one going to Oban on the south side of the village, the other north to Fort William where the station platform waiting room had been converted into the admin office for the gold mine company.

As he climbed the hill and looked back, he could see the remains of what had been various dumps of shale, perhaps from original lead mine workings. Parts of the hillside looked dreadful where vegetation and trees no longer grew. What a shame, thought Peter. No wonder the Highlands and Islands Development people were so protective of allowing large scale mining to take place.

Maybe the lower branch line had once been used to carry lead-bearing rock away for processing in those early days and Peter made a mental note to find out.

Back down in the village he arrived just in time to see the Dutch coach departing. To Peter, it looked as if this time every seat was occupied! Surely he could not have been mistaken when he watched the passengers alight. Or maybe the simple answer was they had been dropped off somewhere on the way to Tyndrum?

Over a cup of tea sitting in The Green Wellie café, he phoned the Loch Achray hotel and having introduced himself, Peter asked if the Manager was available.

A familiar voice came on the line and said, "Hello Mr. Kingston. How can I help you" Peter explained he had now moved on to the Inversnaid hotel for two nights and was composing yet another tourist article. "I know you have a regular visit by Dutch tourists, but do you ever have any other overseas visitors. He was told generally "No" as the hotel was often usually fully booked by Lochs and Glens clients.

"Are the Dutch coaches always full," asked Peter in a casual way. "Yes, the Scottish Highlands are providing very popular and the coach with us for the next five days - having arrived last night - does not have a single spare seat," said the Manager.

Peter thanked him for his help and repeated how much he had enjoyed his Loch Achray stay.

Sitting back to enjoy his cup of tea, Peter mulled over the unusual Dutch coach situation. He was convinced it had been only about two thirds full when it parked up but full again on leaving The Green Wellie.

He drove back down the road to Crianlarich and then towards Callander but before reaching that town he came to a road junction indicating Loch Earn. He decided to turn off and headed along the Loch, spotting a sign for

Crieff and whisky distillery. "Another tourist place to highlight," thought Peter.

At the local tourist office Peter collected various brochures. One told him there was a cut glass factory, other contained the history of the area and a third was all about the Famous Grouse whisky distillery.

"Enough here for an entire article", thought Peter.

He did not want to be late back as he had promised his Editor, Bert, there would another travel article on its way by the end of the day.

He returned along the same road to Lochearnhead, turned left towards Callander and then decided as it was sunny and clear to spoil himself once again with a trip over the Rob Roy Pass to Aberfoyle before turning onto the single-track road to the Inversnaid hotel.

Back in his room he washed his hands, made a cup of tea and took a biscuit from a packet which had been left on his tray. Opening his laptop, he allowed his thoughts to embrace not only what he had seen on his drive today but more about the area around Loch Lomond and the Inversnaid hotel.

There was no problem in occasionally repeating himself in the articles, thought Peter. So much of the Scottish Highlands were worth repeating to people down south. It was stunning scenery with so much to take in.

His mobile rang and it was his Editor. "Hello Peter, how has your day gone at Loch Lomond?" Peter described his morning and then asked Bert if there had been any further jewellery theft developments.

Bert told him there were no new leads so Peter asked if he could bounce his own theory off his Editor.

"Fire away Peter. Is this another one of your gut feelings?" Peter said he was going to repeat an idea he had suggested a few days ago. "I have a theory that the jewellery shop thefts are not only being carried out by overseas criminals, but they are coming into the UK disguised as overseas tourists. I also believe however ridiculous and fanciful it might seem the Scottish Highlands are involved but not necessarily the Scottish gold mine."

There was silence for a few minutes from the other end before Bert replied. "Somehow, Peter. I do not think you are a million miles from the truth, but it is making the connection. Have you any further thoughts on how they might be achieving it," asked Bert.

Peter put forward the theory they came into the UK as tourists, perhaps on coaches from Holland or similar, some got off the coach at strategic locations around England whichever route a particular coach was taking, and those passengers were then replaced by others who had been here for weeks or perhaps even months so that when the coach left on the ferry, maybe from Harwich, they had the full quota of passengers the coach had arrived with.

You see, Bert," explained Peter. "They might come in on a Dutch coach, but they are maybe not Dutch at all. What if they were temporarily living in Holland having migrated from another eastern bloc country, made use as tourists of a regular coach route into the UK and then switched with those already here? Maybe they even manage to take some gold out with them, but it would need melting down using an extremely hot furnace before being moved."

Bert whistled. "You should write a crime novel, Peter. It sounds a terrific but a very unlikely real-life scenario."

Peter decided not to pursue the idea with his Editor, especially when Bert asked about future travel articles and the next Advertorial. The next travel article would be sent overnight and as Peter was moving to Loch Tummel north of Pitlochry the following day, it would be about Wednesday for the next and final Advertorial.

Bert said that would be fine. "Joking apart, Peter, I will put your theory to the detective Superintendent leading the jewellery thefts in the Home Counties region and see what his reaction is I will let you know either tomorrow evening or Tuesday morning."

With that the call ended, Peter sat down to write and promised himself to phone Fiona before his dinner at 7pm.

CHAPTER

15

Their phone call had lasted half an hour and they talked about being together at the end of the week for a romantic weekend. Peter reminded Fiona he had an early start and a long drive to the Loch Tummel hotel beyond Pitlochry.

"The days will pass quickly, Fiona, but I must get the final advertising article written for the hotel company and I want to write at least one more travel article. Scotland has so much to offer," he told her.

After that he slept soundly and happily.

The next morning it was an early breakfast and after thanking the Manager and staff at Reception, Peter set off towards the A9 and north to Pitlochry.

Meanwhile, back down south Peter's Editor and joined the conference with Home Counties senior detectives to review all the cases and what evidence, if any, existed to try and find a link between the various thefts of gold from the numerous jewellery shops.

Bert put forward Peter's theory that foreign criminals, disguised as tourists, were entering the UK and had become organised into a gang located at strategic points throughout England.

One senior detective said they had themselves been thinking along similar lines, but it was knowing where to start. He told the conference that Immigration officials had said it was virtually impossible to stop and question every tourist.

Bert said his News Editor, Peter, had put forward the theory that Dutch tourists were involved but the detective assured him the Dutch were some of the UK's closest and friendliest European partners.

The senior Immigration official agreed and said some spot checks had been made in recent weeks but nothing untoward had come to light. He told the meeting that it was more likely an international gang, hitherto unknown in the UK, had managed to establish itself and were responsible for the spate of robberies.

The Conference broke up without drawing any firm conclusions, but all agreed extra vigilance would be stepped up and MI5 and MI6 would be asked to help.

Meanwhile Peter's journey up the A9 had been relaxing and uneventful; and soon he saw a sign for Pitlochry, so he decided to visit the town for a coffee before seeking the road to Loch Tummel.

He was pleasantly surprised to see a comprehensive range of shops including a well-stocked butchers and general stores. There was a pharmacy and several tourist related shops selling Scottish woollens as well as a bakery which had a good selection of cakes and pastries together with several tea and coffee shops.

Parking was no problem and he managed to pull up outside one of them without difficulty. He went in and was warmly welcomed as he selected one of the small tables covered in a nice clean white linen tablecloth. A young Scottish lass came over and he ordered a coffee and a buttered scone.

"Would you like jam," she asked in a broad Scottish accent. "We make our own from locally grown strawberries," she told Peter.

He said that would be nice and as she disappeared off with his order, Peter looked around and studied some of the photos and paintings hanging on the café walls. There were Scottish lochs and mountains, waterfalls and deer including one photograph of a magnificent stag. The waitress noticed Peter looking and she told him they were lucky enough to have a wildlife photographer living close by who had taken that picture and many others which were often sold in one of the local shops.

The owner of the café came over and Peter introduced himself and said he was on his way to the Loch Tummel hotel for a two-night stay and was looking for places of interest that could be included in his articles.

He was told that in one direction he would find Balmoral Castle, home to the Royal Family when they were in Scotland while in the opposite direction was the home of the Duke of Atholl who the only individual in the UK that is entitled to have a private army.

"Gosh" said Peter out loud. "Now that is really something worth including."

Having finished his food and drink, Peter left feeling refreshed but before he had reached his car, his Editor Bert was on the phone. "Peter there has been yet another jewellery shop raid. This time it is in your turf, a small town called Moffet. It is apparently a tourist hot spot, no useful CCTV in the town and it happened just before shops were opening. At this stage Police Scotland have no clues but dozens of holiday coaches pull up there as there as a large shopping centre on the edge of town."

Bert asked Peter to keep an ear to the ground and then asked how his final visit to Loch Tummel was going.

"I am just on my way to the hotel now. I stopped at a delightful small place called Pitlochry and it is very close to Blair Castle which is a story in itself as the Duke of Atholl has his own army. I plan to try and arrange a visit tomorrow," he told Bert. " Sounds good Peter. Don't let this gold thing distract you but I have a feeling you could be onto something with this Scottish gold mine. Just do not get involved in anything rash without speaking to me first," said Bert. With that, the phone went dead.

Peter drove off, rejoined the A9 but within a short distance he saw the turn off to the left on a fairly narrow, winding road indication the direction to Tummel Bridge. Peter was surprised with the narrowness of the road and how it twisted and turned. He spotted a large stretch of water and guessed that was Loch Tummel. Eventually he came to a junction indicating the Loch Tummel hotel. On the opposite side of the road was a small power station and a small collection of cottages and opposite that was the entrance to the hotel's car park.

At Reception Peter introduced himself and soon the Manager, Campbell, appeared and told Peter he was expected. I will have you shown to your room and if there is anything you require just let me or the receptionist know," he told Peter.

Peter immediately asked if the hotel had any information on Blair Castle. "Yes, we do have a brochure which you can borrow, and you are also in luck because tomorrow there will be rehearsals for the forthcoming Highland Games," said Campbell.

Once inside his first-floor room Peter marvelled at the impressive views of Loch Tummel and the sweep of the surrounding hills. Before unpacking he rang Fiona who answered almost immediately.

"Hi. I have arrived," said Peter.

"Thought you might have said how much you missed me," said Fiona giggling.

"Very much so, as well you know," said Peter trying to sound serious. But they then both laughed together, and Fiona said it would not be long until Friday.

Peter told her about his journey and the stop-off at Pitlochry. "Tomorrow I am going to visit Blair Castle and if I have time I might drive on to Balmoral. But I only have tomorrow to see everything and get my next article written and approved before I leave the following morning," he said.

Peter told Fiona of his plan to return via Tydrum. "Did you read or hear about the jewellery raid at Moffet?" He told her he was still convinced the gold mine had some connection with all the gold and jewellery raids in the past few months. "The raid at Moffat is the first in Scotland and every raid seems to have been working northwards throughout England and the various police forces involved seemed baffled. There do not appear to be any leads," said Peter.

Fiona told him that if he was going to return to Tyndrum before meeting her to be very careful. "From your previous record you seem to have a habit of getting yourself involved up to your neck. Oh Peter, please do not do anything stupid. I am so looking forward to seeing you again on Friday."

Peter promised but also said he would phone later that evening after dinner for another chat if that was ok.

Fiona said it was always ok. "I love hearing your voice when we cannot be together," she said.

The call ended and Peter unpacked. He decided to go back down to Reception and collect the information on Blair Athol before showering and having dinner.

Back down at Reception Peter was given a brochure on Blair Castle from which he learned the castle had been in the same Atholl family for over seven centuries. So, for the past 750 years the castle has changed and adapted to the needs of the time. Peter read that from Mary Queen of Scots to the Civil War; then the battle of Culloden and to Queen Vitoria and her love of the Highlands, so much so that she presented Colours to the Atholl Highlanders.

Fascinating, thought Peter. That was definitely his first port of call the next morning.

He had read that although the Atholl Highlanders were not an official part of the British Army they were formed as a private military unit to protect the Duke of Atholl and the Regiments duties were these days purely ceremonial. The Duke was the Chieftain of Clan Murray.

As the evening meal was arranged for 7pm Peter decided to shave, shower and start drafting his advertorial article on Tummel Bridge. In many ways it was quite different from the other places he had visited; the long narrow and twisting approach road; the hills as distinct from high mountains and apart from the small collection of cottages, quite removed from any large towns although Pitlochry seemed interesting and to perhaps have more beneath the surface than first appeared.

Loch Tummel was 11km in length with a large dam at the Pitlochry end and was attraction for tens of thousands of annual visitors. There was a viewing area known as the Queens View which many people believed had been named after Queen Victoria. But Peter learned from the brochure it had originally been named after Queen Isabel, wife of Robert the Bruce, in the 14th century. Peter thought he would visit both the Dam and the viewing point the following day after his visit to Blair Castle.

Enough research, time for a meal, said Peter to himself.

He selected Scotch broth; fish with boiled potatoes and broccoli, followed by cheese and biscuits. It was all washed down with a glass of Shiraz.

Back in his room, Peter phoned Fiona and their conversation moved quickly to more intimate discussions of their forthcoming time together at the weekend. There was no repeat of the Tyndrum Gold Mine.

Their call lasted 20 minutes and Peter was told by Fiona she had an early start the next day and they could speak longer the following evening when Peter could tell her all about his day. Peter watched the TV news and quickly fell asleep with dreams of Fiona rather than gold.

The next morning Peter showered and enjoyed an early full Scottish breakfast. It was going to be a long day, he thought. The Manager, Campbell, was at Reception and Peter told him his plan for the day.

"I think you will find it interesting, especially the Blair Castle rehearsals. Balmoral is probably a drive too far and there is not much to see from the road. Security is tight and stopping along that stretch is not encouraged. I can give you any details on Balmoral later if you want them Peter," said Campbell.

Peter noticed from his road map that instead of driving back down Loch Tummel to the A9 he could use a cross country route to Blair Castle which would give him a better chance of enjoying the scenery.

It was a 45-minute journey and the route avoided the main A9 road from Perth to Inverness.

At the Castle gate he stopped and paid the entry charge and was directed to the car parking area.

Armed with his camera Peter made his way to a grassed area in front of the outstanding castle structure. There was already quite a crowd, no doubt from several coaches which Peter had noticed at the far end of the car park. Soon about 100 soldiers appeared on parade. Their uniforms were not unlike those worn by regular troops in the British army.

There appeared to be a sergeant-major and an officer giving parade orders and Peter was impressed by the smartness of the part-time soldiers.

After about half an hour the soldiers were dismissed giving Peter the chance to wander over to the Castle entrance and collect an illustrated brochure for a charge of five pounds. He noticed a sign indicating a café and he wandered down a wide corridor and into a small room serving drinks and home-made cakes.

Sitting to one side he read the brochure and was interested to find references to the soldiers being made up of Blair Castle estate workers. They received an additional annual salary for their military activities.

Peter joined a small group being shown around the ground floor of the Castle and various large oil paintings depicting the various Dukes of Blair Atholl over the centuries.

Once the tour was over Peter made his way back to his car and studied his road map. After all it was already lunchtime and he wanted to view the Dam near Pitlochry and also the Queen's View point. He drove down the A9 to Pitlochry on a particular mission.

Once in Pitlochry centre, he parked up and wandered along the pavement to where he had seen a jewellery shop on his previous days' visit. He went inside and a middle-aged gentleman appeared. Peter introduced himself and asked this chap if he was the owner.

The man replied he was, and Peter explained the reasons for his next question.

"Have you read about the numerous jewellery shop raids in England and just a few days ago thieves raided a jewellery shop at Moffat," asked Peter.

The man replied yes and before Peter could ask his next question the shop owner said. "I have already telephoned a CCTV company down the road at Perth at they are coming tomorrow to set up a system which will cover both the inside and external area of my jewellery shop. I have also spoken to our local police constable, and we are all on our toes. I do not want thieves raiding my shop which has been in my family for well over 100 years," he said.

Peter was impressed.

He then asked the jewellery shop owner what he knew about Scottish gold at Tyndrum.

"Ever since it was first discovered there has been considerable coverage in Scottish newspapers and on both radio and television. In the jewellery trade here in Scotland we are particularly interested because Scottish gold is offered to us first and then any over is sold elsewhere in Britain," he told Peter. "It has a special value and is much sought after in the jewellery trade. In all this shop's history we have never once suffered any sort of theft, so it is better to take precautions now before anything like that happens" he said.

Peter told him he was writing a special article for his newspaper down south in Surrey about Tyndrum gold as well as Lochs and Glens.

"We get quite a few of the Tummel hotel guests coming to Pitlochry and some even come into my shop and buy jewellery items which have a Scottish connection. Pitlochry does very well throughout the year from this coach traffic," he said to Peter.

Feeling like a cup of tea and a slice of cake, Peter thanked the man for his help. He gave him a card and in return took the details of the jewellery shop and promised to send the man a copy of the newspaper article about Tummel.

At the café he had visited the previous day he asked for directions to the Pitlochry Dam and having eaten the piece of cake, washed down by the cup of tea Peter drove and parked up in a large car park and followed signs indicating the viewing area.

The Dam was certainly impressive, and Peter made notes. Construction had begun in 1947 and was completed in the early 1950's. The scheme had been controversial with many people believing the Dam would lead to rivers and the small stream drying up. There were also fears over salmon spawning in the river, but a fish-ladder had been incorporated into the project. The Loch Tummel Dam was one of over 40 hydro-electric schemes for Scotland.

It was certainly an impressive structure and attracted more than 600,000 visitors a year.

Peter's final port of call on his way back to the hotel was The Queen's View, a short distance along the winding road leading to Tummel Bridge. When he arrived the small car park was already busy, but Peter managed to squeeze into a small space beneath some trees.

The view was certainly spectacular and no wonder it had been viewed by Queen Victoria in 1866. Loch Tummel stretched out before him and according to the information displayed, it was one of the most photographed views in the whole of Scotland. It was set in the Tay Forest Park and offered views to Schiehallion, affectionately known as "The Fairy Mountain". Also, in the distance on a clear day could be seen the mountains of Glen Coe.

Peter certainly had more than enough to write about for his final advertorial which he needed to complete as soon as he got back and well before dinner. Tomorrow would be an exciting day with a return to Tyndrum and to find out more about gold mine. He had made up his mind that if there was a connection between the gold jewellery robberies and this Scottish gold mine, he would find it.

Back at the Tummel hotel Peter was greeted at Reception and asked if he had enjoyed his day. He replied that it had been very informative and said he had managed to see the main tourist attractions. Once in his room he phoned Bert and told him the advertorial article would be finished that evening and would email it through and also send it to Alison at Lochs and Glens.

"Are there any developments in the jewellery raid investigations," he asked Bert who told him the police thought they had a lead which was being followed up by Police Scotland.

"Get your witing finished, Peter. Leave the theft of gold to the authorities. After all you are due on that train from Glasgow Central to London on Monday and we are all looking forward to seeing you here in the office."

With that, the line went dead. Peter got out his laptop and started writing. An hour later, he was more than satisfied with the article so he sent it through to Alison and decided to have a much needed shower and then he could speak to Fiona. Tomorrow was Thursday and he would be seeing her Friday morning for what he hoped would be a romantic three-day weekend at Loch Lomond.

The evening meal was the usual high standard. Peter had opted for Leek and Cauliflower soup followed by roast chicken breast and for dessert it was one of his favourites, treacle sponge pudding.

The glass of Australian Merlot had been really nice, and he rounded off the meal with a coffee in the lounge, offering superb views along Loch Tummel.

After this he went up to his room and phoned Fiona.

"I am so missing you, Peter. Friday morning cannot come soon enough."

Peter told her he felt the same and he was sure their three days together in the romantic setting of Loch Lomond would be wonderful. Peter explained that Police Scotland had a new lead in the jewellery raid at Moffat.

"Oh Peter. Please try and put this gold thing out of your mind and just concentrate on us. You seem more fixated with gold than me," she said.

"Well. The two might well go together one day," giggled Peter.

"Oh, you are a tease, but it sounds promising," Fiona replied.

Their conversation ended with Peter promising to phone the next day when he got to Tyndrum. "I just want to convince myself there is nothing there to link it with the jewellery thefts. I sometimes get a gut feeling about something which needs following up," he told Fiona.

About ten minutes after their call had ended Peter's phone rang. It was Alison from Lochs and Glens.

"I did try calling before Peter, but your line was busy. I just wanted to say I have read your latest article and, as always, it is fine. No changes are necessary, but I really want to thank you for your various writings. You have a good eye and understanding for what needs highlighting and I am sure the various articles accompanying our advertising will bring us many more customers," said Alison.

Peter soon dropped off to sleep with happy thoughts of his time to come with Fiona.

CHAPTER

16

Before leaving Loch Tummel Peter studied a local map and found there was a quicker cross-country route back to Tyndrum avoiding the need to journey back down the busy A9. He had enjoyed an early breakfast so before mid-morning he was at the gold mine village and he parked up at the Green Wellie car park and went inside for a much needed comfort break.

As he came out he spotted a familiar face. It was Alistair from The Highland hotel at Fort William.

"Hello", said Peter. Alistair seemed quite taken aback and at first did not recognise Peter. But then he realised who it was and said. "Hi, I thought you had gone to Loch Tummel for the rest of your writing?"

Peter told Alistair that he had been, written and decided to return to Tyndrum to learn more about the gold mine. "I am fascinated to learn that Scotland has so much gold in its mountains. People from England have probably no idea. They just think of Scotland as a beautiful country with mountains and lochs. But never of gold mines," he said.

Alistair seemed flustered and certainly did not want to talk so he made his excuse for leaving. "Enjoy the rest of your visit, Peter." And with that he walked off in the direction of the car park.

Peter made his way up the road through Tyndrum and spotted a group of white cottages on the edge of the village. Opposite was the general store Peter had visited on his first visit to Tyndrum when he had asked about the gold mine. The shop also sold newspapers and cards, so Peter went in and introduced himself. It was a different person behind the counter which made life a little easier.

"I am trying to find out a little more of the history and how old original parts of the village might be," he asked the lady behind the counter. She told Peter there had been a small community ever since the first lead mine had opened several hundred years ago. "There has been mining in this area for centuries and small traces of gold found in the streams and rivers running down from these mountains for as long as people can recall," she told Peter.

He purchased a Scottish daily newspaper and a bar of chocolate, thanked the lady for her help and was about to step out of the shop when he saw Alistair accompanied by two men heading into one of the cottages down a lane opposite.

He went back into the shop and apologised for returning so soon. "What are those cottages opposite and who lives there now?" he asked.

The lady told him they were some of the original miners' cottages and the bottom two were owned by people from abroad and used as holiday homes. "We locals do not like the idea of our homes being brought up by people from abroad. Young Scottish folk need homes but there is little we can do when property is sold on the open market. Those two went for well above their market value," she said.

Peter thanked her again and as he left, he saw Alistair and the two men leaving. One of them appeared to be carrying a large circular object, which

Peter thought he recognised. "Strange," thought Peter. "Why would they be carrying a wheel hub cap?"

He watched them heading towards the car park but kept discreetly out of sight. Peter thought he recognised one of the men as the Dutch coach driver he had seen at Loch Achray. The reason was soon revealed. There was the Dutch coach parked at the far end of the car park and the men began replacing the wheel hub on the front off-side coach wheel. Alistair shook hands and began walking back in Peter's direction, so he ducked into the Green Wellie shop and pretended to be looking at shelves of Scottish souvenirs.

Alistair went straight to the café and then sat down with a cup of coffee. Peter pretended to be so surprised to see Alistair again.

"Well, hello. "Twice in one day" and before Alistair had recovered from the shock of seeing Peter again, and so soon after their initial meeting, Peter sat down and said he was going to research the history of the original lead mines and the Scottish miners.

He asked Alistair if he liked the Green Wellie shop and the village of Tyndrum. Alistair seemed initially lost for words and then explained it was a convenient stop between Fort William and the Lochs and Glens head office near Loch Lomond.

"I expect you have got to know a few of the local inhabitants," said Peter in an enquiring voice.

Alistair replied that he really never had time to stop for long chats. "I stop for a comfort break, a quick cup of coffee and then I head off in whichever direction," he said. "Now I really must be going. I have to be back at Fort William hotel before the first sitting for the evening meal. Goodbye Peter". And with that he stood up and left. Peter sat for a while and decided to phone Fiona. Her voice mail was on so he left a message to say he was at

Tyndrum and would call again later. "Just remind me to tell you about wheel hub caps." Peter smiled to himself. That will keep her guessing.

Then, allowing his curiosity to get the better of him, he walked up the road, crossed over to the cottages and wandered down to the last cottage where the three men had appeared from.

The end one of the two backed onto the wooded area at both the side and rear. Nobody appeared at home. There were no signs of life, no obvious windows open but smoke was coming out of the chimney. Peter noticed a small rear door which he gently pushed, and it creaked open. Peering inside there was a small old fashioned wooden table and three chairs. Dirty plates littered the table and a half-eaten loaf was on the side with a jar of Scottish marmalade. There was an old solid looking fireside chair but otherwise the room was sparse. No pictures hung on the walls and a sort of whitewash had been applied to the originally plastered walls.

On one wall was a lovely but small old-fashioned fireplace. It was still glowing with smoke coming from a half-burned log. The floor was tiled but beneath the table appeared to be a trap door. Peter was curious. He knew it was probably not advisable, but he pulled it open, and a wood step ladder led down to goodness knows what. Peter was about to close it up when he heard a car crunch to a halt in the lane outside. He took a quick peek and much to his shock and horror, it was Alistair.

With no way out, Peter's only choice was to disappear down the ladder and into what was perhaps a cellar. He carefully pulled the trap door down behind him and he listened.

Footsteps above.

Something heavy was being dragged across the floor. Shortly afterwards another heavy item was also being dragged into the cottage on the floor above Peter's head. Footsteps again, this time a door was slammed shut and

Peter thought he heard a key turning in a lock and a car being reversed up the lane.

After what seemed an age Peter climbed the ladder in the darkness and tried to raise the trap door. But as much as he tried the door would not budge. Peter was trapped in darkness and in cold. He tried his phone but there was no signal. But the phone did have plenty of battery, so Peter switched on the phone's torch and climbed back down the ladder.

Time to investigate his surroundings. Perhaps there was another way out, thought Peter.

The dim light revealed Peter was standing in quite a large space and what appeared to be some sort of tunnel led off to the left. He searched for any form of lighting or a light switch but initially drew a blank.

Peter had never been one for getting into a panic, but this situation seemed fairly hopeless. He appeared to have two choices. To sit it out until someone returned to the cottage but how long might that be. Perhaps a day, even a week and then come face to face from what could be some unsavoury characters.

The alternative would be to investigate where the tunnel led to. But it might go on for a long way and Peter's phone torch would not last forever. Crikey, not a good outlook at all!

He decided to explore the tunnel for a short distance. Under foot it was smooth and appeared well used but in places water trickled down the dark walls. As he walked, he realised the tunnel was beginning to turn to the right and there were several places where it appeared miners had attempted to make new tunnels to both the left and right.

He had gone several hundred yards when suddenly dim lights came on illuminating the passageway ahead and he could hear voices. He froze then gathered his thoughts and ducked into one of the openings which had obviously been intended as a new tunnel.

The voices grew louder, and their language was certainly not English. Peter pushed himself back into the recess as far as he could and put his arm over his face so that it did not shine out against the blackness.

The men, Peter thought there were either two or three, went past in the direction he had come from, and they had disappeared round the bend in the tunnel. When Peter judged it safe, he came out from his hiding place and decided to investigate the direction the men had appeared from. It was hopeful to him the men must have got into the tunnel from another entrance.

Peter carefully made his way further along the dimly lit tunnel. It seemed to go on and on but after a while the light appeared to get stronger. There was a smell of a fire and more voices.

Rounding yet another bend Peter was shocked and amazed to see a group of men around what was obviously a red-hot furnace above which hung a large pot. He had only a few seconds to seek out somewhere to hide before his presence was likely to be discovered. Fortunately, there was another recess where even more of the rock had been dug out and Peter was able to conceal himself safely yet continue to observe what was happening a little further along.

The men were placing items from a suitcase into the large pot. Straining his eyes Peter thought he could make out watch chains, bracelets and smaller items. Wow! Could these be gold jewellery stolen from various shops - but how on earth did it finish up here in the Scottish Highlands?

At least he had his connection.

Peter just had time to squeeze back into his concealed hiding place when the men who had passed him earlier returned, each carrying a large and obviously heavy suitcase.

There were lots of discussions in between peering into the large pot. After a short time one of the men produced a hub cap, similar to the one Peter had seen the other men taking to the coach in the Green Wellie car park. Placing it onto a bench at one side of the central area Peter watched as one of the men cleaned out the inside of the wheel hub cap and then one of the other men carefully poured some of the liquid into it while a third man appeared to be carefully spreading it round.

So that was it, thought Peter. Melt down the gold items, pour a thin layer into hub caps. But if the authorities on either side of the Channel were searching for hidden gold, surely this would stand out.

His question was soon answered when one of the other men appeared with a spray can and began spraying what appeared to be a dark colour over the gold surface.

Ingenious, thought Peter.

The men continued with their work, appearing to sort through items from the cases and occasionally putting more items into the pot. Peter had noticed the fire was fuelled by what appeared to be industrial gas canisters, as tall as a man.

There surely must be another entrance, he thought to himself, they wouldn't carry those down that ladder.

Carefully shielding the light from his phone Peter looked at his watch and was aghast to see it was after 4pm. How much longer was he going to have to remain in his hiding place?

Peter realised he was hungry, so he carefully and quietly broke himself off some chocolate. It tasted so good. But he had nothing to drink and there was no water readily available.

The hours dragged by. The men continued with their work and Peter had started to nod off, uncomfortably leaning against the cold rock. But there was nowhere to sit, and he had to be careful not to make any noise and be discovered.

But nod off he did and when Peter woke up, it was to pitch darkness. At first, he thought he had problems with his eyes as there was nothing to focus on. But there was no sound apart from the occasional drip of water. The hot fire had been extinguished so carefully taking out his phone Peter switched on the torch. The light was dim and there was a warning on the screen. Battery low.

Oh hell. This was all he needed.

He crept out from the recess and hugging the tunnel wall he began to walk and walk, only occasionally using his phone torch which was now quickly fading. There was some fresh air coming from somewhere but no shafts of light to give Peter a clue. His watch showed it was well after 9pm and hopefully Fiona would be getting really worried about his disappearance.

But he had no way of letting anyone know where he was, or that he was well – so far.

CHAPTER

17

Peter was right. Fiona had become so worried she had started to make enquiries. Just where was her beloved Peter? She had contacted the Green Wellie shop by phone. No, they did not recall anyone answering Peter's description, but they would ask around. Fiona left the manageress her personal phone number.

She next contacted Police Scotland, but they told her they really could not instigate a Missing Person enquiry because he had only been "out of contact" for a short period of time and they were sure there was a simple explanation like his mobile phone's battery had run out.

Fiona decided to take matters into her own hands and drove straight from work to Tyndrum. It was well after 8pm and dark when she arrived. She phoned her mother to say where she was and why. "Try not to worry dear, I am sure there will be a rational explanation," said her mother.

Fiona went into the Green Wellie café which was about to close. Nobody had any news. She went to the main hotel but nobody with Peter's name had checked in. She tried several B&B's but again drew a blank. Where could she turn to? Fiona had parked near the petrol filling station and drove from one end of Tyndrum to the other. Perhaps he had decided to book in somewhere else but which direction. Fiona's choice was to head back down the road towards Crianlarich. There was a large hotel and several smaller B&Bs and it was in the direction of home. It was getting on for 10pm when she eventually went through her own front door. Her Mother was waiting with a cup of tea, some warm soup and a soothing "try not to worry, Fiona. There will be an explanation."

Fiona sat down exhausted. Her mind was in turmoil and what was happening was so out of character. Peter was a kind, loving person and took every opportunity to phone her. He said he was in Tyndrum so where could he had driven to and why had he not contacted her?

The television was on and she became distracted by the News at Ten. The newsreader was giving details of the jewellery shop raid at Moffat and said there had been developments. Next was a Police Scotland superintendent who said the Police were following up new information based on dashcam footage from a local resident's car. It showed from behind two men coming out of an alleyway where there was a side door to the jewellery shop. Local police had entered and found the jewellery shop owner tied and gagged in an upstairs room. Being elderly, he was in a state of shock and had been taken to hospital and so far, had been unable to help with any description of the assailants, other than to say he believed they had spoken a few words in a foreign language.

Fiona began to realise that perhaps what Peter had been saying was right after all. Gold, Scotland, foreign people involved. But that did not explain why Peter had not been in touch.

Fiona told her mother she was phoning Police Scotland in Glasgow again and to tell them that her boyfriend, Peter, a journalist from England, believed the numerous jewellery raids throughout England and now one in Scotland were all linked and that perhaps the gold mine at Tyndrum was implicated.

She got through only to be told all senior officers had now gone home but her comments would be put on the Chief Superintendents desk first thing in the morning. Perhaps Peter's disappearance at Tyndrum might be connected after all.

By breakfast time Friday morning phones were ringing between Police Scotland and London where police, HM Customs and Immigration and other involved Agencies had been coordinating all information. South and east coast ports were alerted from Dover and the Channel Tunnel to Harwich and Felixstowe and as far north as Hull.

Scottish local police had been despatched from Oban and Crianlarich to begin a house-to-house search in the area around Tyndrum. Meanwhile the dashcam footage was being studied in minute detail and police from Dumfries were in the town of Moffat seeing if there were any more leads.

Fiona was up early and after a cup of coffee and a slice of toast she headed back towards Tyndrum, telling her mother that she would keep in touch. "If Peter should phone here, please phone me immediately mum but find out where he is calling from," said Fiona.

She arrived at Tyndrum to find the Green Wellie shop already busy and the car park more than half full, so she had to drive towards the rear to find a parking space. As she got out and began to walk towards the café she spotted an Enterprise hire car. Her heart began to pound. Could it be Peters; she looked more closely at the car and the registration plate and immediately realised it was the car which had been booked out to Peter when he first arrived at Glasgow several weeks ago.

Fiona tried the doors which were all locked. She peered inside. No luggage, no clues so where was Peter? She walked towards the café entrance just as two policemen were coming out.

"Excuse me," said Fiona. The men stopped and looked at her. "Are you looking for a man called Peter Kingston?"

"And who might you be young lady," enquired the senior of the two who had sergeants' stripes on his jacket. Fiona explained she worked for Enterprise car rental at Glasgow Airport and she had been responsible for the car loan. Since then, she had spent quite a bit of time with Peter Kingston and they had kept in touch daily by phone.

"Have you indeed. And why are you concerned now?" he asked.

Fiona told him about yesterday's phone message from Peter saying he had arrived in Tyndrum and that they were due to meet up this morning and spend a few days at Loch Lomond.

The men looked at each other and smiled. "I see. And why do you want to speak to us now?" said the other officer.

"I have just found Peter's Enterprise car," she said.

Her statement left both policemen looking both surprised and a little shocked.

"Can you show us please," said the senior officer. And together she led them back through the car park to where Peter's car was parked.

The Sergeant was on his phone explaining what had been discovered. Fiona heard him saying something about "no signs of anything suspicious. And the car being locked and nothing visible inside."

After a brief conversation the officer asked Fiona if she could recall anything else.

"The voice mail Peter Kingston left on my phone asked me to remind him to tell me about wheel hub caps," she told the officer. He wrote some notes down in his book including her mobile phone number and said the

Police would get back to her in due course.

With that, they left.

Meanwhile, back at the Fort William hotel Alistair had heard on the radio news about the missing journalist in the Tyndrum area and a police search taking place. He rang the local police, introduced himself and after outlining the reason for his call, was put through to a senior officer.

He explained he had been passing through Tyndrum and spotted Peter Kingston at the Green Wellie shop. "As he had been staying at our hotel a few days ago I thought it strange he was back at Tyndrum as he said he was going to Loch Tummel when he left us," he explained.

"Peter Kingston said he had been there, written his article and had returned to Tyndrum on his way to Loch Lomond as he wanted to get some history on the original lead mines in the Tyndrum area. I left him at the café as I had to get back here to the hotel," said Alistair.

The officer at the other end of the phone thanked him for coming forward. "Your information may or may not be of any help. But we will keep you aware of any developments."

The call ended and Alistair felt he had done his duty without possibly incriminating himself in any way with Peter's disappearance.

The report Alistair had given, together with Fiona's statement to the officers at Tyndrum went through to the desk of the senior officer at Glasgow coordinating all information about the Moffat jewellery shop raid, information on any possible suspicious-speaking foreigners, together with what appeared to be an unrelated disappearance of a missing journalist at Tyndrum.

But one sentence had caught his eye and he mulled over in his mind what it might mean and if it had any significance.

Wheel hub caps.

Down south, Bert was about to leave his office and enjoy a relaxing weekend at home in his garden when his phone rang. Hesitating he just wanted to get away from the hustle and bustle of the newspaper and enjoy some quiet time with his family. Picking up the phone, he said "Yes".

He was asked if he was the Editor to which he again answered "Yes". The next few words were about to change his life and thoughts of a quiet weekend. "Yes, I do employ a journalist by the name of Peter Kingston. Why, has something dreadful happened to him. He was on a writing assignment in the Scottish Highlands."

This is Police Scotland and I am calling from Glasgow. I am afraid your Mr Kingston has gone missing in what might be suspicious circumstances. His hire car has been found abandoned in a small village called Tyndrum. Have you heard of it, Sir?"

Bert's heart sank. Oh no! "Is that where they have a gold mine?" he asked.

The voice at the other end of the phone sounded a little surprised and said, "Why yes, how do you know about it, Sir?"

Bert explained about Peter Kingston's theory that it was somehow connected to the many jewellery shop raids across England and the one at Moffat in Scotland. "I told him to stick to his travel writing and not to get mixed up in anything to do with gold mines," said Bert.

"At this stage, Sir, there is no suggestion that Mr Kingston has been near the gold mine or that his apparent disappearance has anything to do with the mine, gold or anything else which is obvious at this stage. Police Scotland is investigating every possibility, and we are trying to keep all interested parties in the loop," said the officer.

Bert thanked him and knew his weekend would have to be re-planned. He called in one of the senior journalists from the newsroom and having explained what had happened in Scotland, asked him to make contact with a newspaper in the area and get some co-operation lined up.

Meanwhile Fiona's comment about wheel hub caps from Peter was being studied with more thought by those agencies in London involved in the numerous jewellery shop thefts.

Perhaps, and only perhaps, items of gold were being concealed in vehicle hub caps. But were they being smuggled out of the country or just moved around the country. Or did it mean something quite different.

Certainly puzzling.

CHAPTER

18

The day wore on with the police seemingly getting nowhere. Another conference was held at police HQ in Glasgow and it was decided, after sifting through all the evidence and statements again, to re-interview some key witnesses. A call was put through to Fort William police requesting they speak again to the Manager of the Fort William hotel about his conversation with Peter Kingston at Tyndrum and exactly where he had last seen him.

Fiona, meanwhile, was in tears and shaking with worry. "Oh, Peter. Peter, why did you have to go back to Tyndrum?" she realised how deeply in love with him she was. Going into the little general store at the far end of the village for a pack of tissues it was a different person behind the counter.

"You poor dear, you look quite upset. Is everything alright?"

Fiona introduced herself and said she was at her wits end of know what had happened to her boyfriend, Peter Kingston.

The lady said she had not been at the shop when the police had visited making enquiries. "I have told them he was asking about the history of lead mines and those little white former miners cottages across the road. Quite weird the comings and goings," she told Fiona. "They were purchased last year by some foreign people and some weeks there seems a lot of activity, then nothing for days. Sometimes you see a foreign car parked in the lane. But I do not understand car registration plates, but this one has an NL sticker on the back. Occasionally there is a black car with a Scottish number plate."

To Fiona, this was really helpful and something quite positive. "If the police return to ask you more questions, please tell them what you have told me," she said.

With that, and having paid for the tissues, Fiona crossed the road and walked towards the row of small white cottages. She stood and looked for a while but there seemed no sign of activity or life. No smoke coming from any chimney, so she slowly walked down the lane peering in windows. She got to the bottom and it was obvious a car had been there are the wheel marks had been left in the soft gravel.

She knocked on the front door but did not expect a reply. Fiona walked round to where there was a side door. It was locked and as she began walking back up the track a car pulled it. Fiona recognised from the number plates it was from Holland. It pulled up alongside her, the window opened and a man in a stern voice but obviously foreign asked her what she was doing.

Fiona explained her boyfriend was missing and she was just knocking on doors making enquiries. "He is not here so please go away. We do not like visitors. Just quiet time which is why we brought these cottages," he said but his accent was certainly not Dutch. It sounded more eastern European.

Fiona made her way back towards the Green Wellie shop and café. Her phone rang and it was her mother. "Why don't you come home Fiona. There is little you can achieve there. I am sure as soon as there is any news you will be contacted," she said.

Fiona promised her mother to think about it. "I am sure a clue to his disappearance has to be here at Tyndrum," she said.

Back at Fort William Alistair was being interviewed again and reminded he had told officers he had briefly met Peter Kingston at the Green Wellie shop. "What did you do after that, sir, asked the officer.

"Well, I drove straight back here. I was on duty at the hotel for the evening meal and the first of our coaches gets back to the hotel with guests between 16.30 and 17.00," said Alistair.

"So, you went nowhere else between the Green Wellie shop and here" asked the officer.

Alistair began to become flustered. Did the Police know something? He bluffed it out.

"No. I drove straight back here officer," he replied.

The policeman thanked him, and he and another officer left.

Why should he mention the connection with the white cottages. Nothing to do with the police, thought Alistair.

But he knew it was a possible clue, but he did not want the police to become involved in what was happening below ground. Alistair had wished right from the start he had not become involved with this international gang of gold jewellery thieves, but he was right in it now, right up to his neck in fact. But they were now blackmailing him and to try and get out now would give the smugglers the opportunity to reveal things Alistair wished to remain secret.

Panic over for now, thought Alistair. But he must try and get out of the mess he was in and should never have offered to help in the first place. Money had been tight and the offer of several thousands of pounds at the time had swayed his judgement. Every time recently he had told this overseas gang he wanted out, he had been threatened with: "Your job is on the line, perhaps far more!"

Back at the Fort William police station the interview report was forwarded by email to Glasgow and collated with all the other interviews and information that had been gathered so far. Copies were emailed down to London.

As Fiona walked back to her car, feeling tired and drained she saw one of the local policemen who was based at Inveraray. He recognised her and walked across. "How are you, Fiona. How is your mother?"

Fiona explained her connection with the police enquiries. "Oh, that explains quite a lot. I had not realised you knew Peter Kingston. This is all a bit of a mystery and some of my colleagues say it could well be mixed up with all the jewellery raids down in England," said officer McCullan.

"Peter kept telling me ever since we first met, he thought there was a connection with thefts of gold in England and the Tyndrum gold mine. When he arrived at Tyndrum he left me a voice message to say he was here and would call later. Since then, there has been nothing. But his car which is on loan from my employer is parked behind the Green Wellie café," said Fiona.

Constable McCullan said he would personally try and keep her informed. "Why don't you go home. There is nothing more you can achieve here," said the policeman.

Fiona decided his advice was sensible. It was the end of the day. She was weary and it was getting cold. She phoned her mother and said she was on her way. "A cup of tea and a warm bath is what I need," she said. But deep down what she really needed was a long, warm hug from Peter. Just where was he and what had happened?

Constable McCullan had driven back to Inveraray and was due for a meeting with the Duke of Argyll on an unrelated matter. At the Castle he was met at the main door and taken into the Duke's private apartments.

He was asked if he had been busy so Constable McCullan outlined his time at Tyndrum helping in the search for Peter Kingston.

"I know that journalist. He has been here to interview me for his travel article. We got talking about gold and the Tyndrum gold mine. He even asked me if there was any gold on my Argyll Estate," said the Duke.

Constable McCullan asked if there had been any surveys. The Duke said there had many, many years ago when his late Father had still been alive. What we do have is a collection of historic maps showing the numerous lead mine workings stretching from Tyndrum towards the edge of our Estate. I believe that over a century ago there were traces of silver found but no records of any large deposits of gold. The Tyndrum gold seam came as quite a pleasant surprise to most people in Scotland. It might have been an even more pleasant surprise to me if the gold seam had been found on my land!" joked the Duke.

He was asked by the policeman if it would be possible to have sight or even loan of the old mine workings? The Duke replied that he could have photo copies made as he was loathe to let historic documents leave the Castle.

Constable McCullan said he quite understood so by the time he had concluded other matters with the Duke, copies of the old maps were available for him to take away.

Once back at the Inveraray police station Constable McCullan phoned through to Glasgow police HQ and gave his report about the meeting with the Fiona, her thoughts on Peter Kingston and he informed the senior officer that he had acquired copies of very old maps showing original lead mine workings.

Constable McCullan said it was always possible Peter Kingston's curiosity had led him into one and fallen down a mine shaft.

"That is certainly a possibility in view of his interest in mines. But the police should keep an open mind at this stage Constable McCullan," said the senior officer. "Yes Sir," he replied, and the phone call ended.

CHAPTER

19

Below ground in his pitch-dark tunnel Peter had no idea of the time of day. His illuminous watch showed 6.30 but was that am or pm. Was it still Friday or was it now Saturday. All he knew was that he was shivering with cold and extremely hungry. He had finished his chocolate hours and hours ago. His clothes felt not only dirty from the tunnel dust but quite damp. It was certainly far from being a dry environment.

What to do next, thought Peter. Do I try and make my way back the way I had come to the cottage, or do I plough on. He could still feel cold, fresh air which must be coming from somewhere. Suddenly the wall turned back to the left. So, this is where the tunnel ends, thought Peter. But where did those other men appear from. And who puts the lights on? So many unanswered questions getting him nowhere fast.

The walls of the tunnel on this side were jagged and Peter knew his skin had been broken in more than one place. But he had to try and find a way out, so he continued, weak as he was, to inch his way along. Suddenly, the wall seemed to end but by feeling the rocks he realised this tunnel wall turned a sharp right. He was about to slowly move round when the dim ceiling lights came on and he heard voices.

There was nowhere to hide so he inched back the way he had come, this time keeping his face towards the tunnel walls. There was less chance of being spotted. The voices grew louder and louder, and he froze as they seemed only feet away. But then the voices grew less obvious and risking a glance he saw the men heading back up the tunnel which Peter thought he must have come along all those hours ago, or could it have been yesterday?

Quickly taking in his surroundings and stock of his position, Peter decided to turn right along the tunnel the men had come from. With the dim ceiling lights on it was so much easier to make progress. He could feel fresh air coming from somewhere ahead. "Just keep going" he said to himself.

He must have travelled at least half a mile and realised the tunnel floor was rising. And then, at last there appeared an opening, hidden by bushes or trees and Peter quickly emerged from his underground tomb.

It was with a huge sigh of relief, and he sat down in the cover of fir trees and undergrowth without realising the ground was wet. He was already wet, his underclothes were clammy, but he did not care. He was free but he must keep his wits about him. What if there were other men around; what if those he had just passed came back?

He decided to stay within the tree cover, but it was so dark, obviously night time and he had no idea which direction to head for. There was no moon so no stars to offer a clue. There was rain in the air but if only he could find something to eat and drink it would help. His lack of energy was slowing any progress and not only making him feel weak, but he was also beginning to get stomach cramp which was a sure sign of lack of liquid intake.

A few hundred yards on he spotted what appeared to be a log cabin. Was there a glow from one of the windows? He edged carefully closer, trying to make sure he did not stand on any broken branches which might crack and cause anyone in the building to investigate.

He came to the edge of the trees, crept along the wooden side of the cabin and carefully peered into the window. There was a half-burnt candle on the table together with a small loaf and one slice cut but untouched. What appeared to be an empty bottle of beer stood on the uncovered wooden table.

The room was empty and although another door led off the space, Peter listened and could not hear any movement or sound so assumed the three men who had passed him in the tunnel had been the occupants. He was so hungry and thirsty surely it was worth the risk to get in, grab the bread and the bottle and get out and back into the protection of the trees as quickly as he could.

Peter had just got hold of the bread and was about to grab the bottle with the other hand when a figure came backwards from the small adjoining room.

Peter rushed back out of the door but inadvertently banged it against the wall as he ran. He went into the forest and just kept moving, twice he stumbled but he could hear a voice shouting something in a language he couldn't comprehend. Peter stood and gasped as quietly as he could for breath. He was still closer to the wooden cabin than he cared to be, but a torch shone out. He kept as hidden as he could behind a tree. After a while the torch light went out, the cabin door slammed shut and Peter breathed a sigh of relief.

That was too close to call, he thought. He stayed put for around ten minutes but tore off some of the bread and swallowed, hardly chewing as he was absolutely famished. The bread was a life saver, Bland but it did not matter. It was food and would give him some energy. Once it was gone Peter thought he would get as much distance between himself and the cabin as he could. Whoever was inside might start a proper search.

From time-to-time Peter stumbled, his clothes becoming more and more torn. He was dirty, covered in rock dust and now green moss and bark scrapings from the trees. On and on he went with no idea whether it was north, south, east or west. Towards or away from Tyndrum? Surely if he could just get moving, he would come to a road or even better, some habitation.

At last, the fir tree forest came to an end and through the gloom Peter thought he could make out some hills and open scrubland. But no roads and no apparent houses. He stumbled on and on, came to the trickle of a stream and bent down to scoop some sweet tasting water. When was the last time he had drunk anything? He drank thirstily but not too quickly. It was like flowing nectar and quite cold. He guessed it was flowing down from high in the heather-covered hills or even snow-capped peaks.

Eventually and taken a little by surprise he came to a rough track. Maybe Forestry Commission or probably some farm. He began to stumble along, dragging his weary feet and conscious that his shoes had now seen better days. The rock-strewn floor of the tunnel had taken its toll.

Eventually he could walk no further. There was a boulder with what appeared to be a patch of smooth grass, so he sat down and soon rolled on his side and fell into a deep sleep.

He awoke to some noise, but he was so delirious from exposure and perhaps hypothermia that he was unaware of the two men and the Land Rover alongside him.

Without offering any resistance Peter was put onto the back seat of the vehicle which then turned round and headed down the hill. Peter and the men arrived at their destination, and he was half carried into a room.

Warmth! Voices. A warm drink was put to his lips and he drank, more asleep than awake.

More voices; his clothes began to be removed and he fell into a deep sleep without realising he was in a warm, comfortable bed and being examined by a doctor.

When he awoke hours later, he opened his eyes. There was a policeman, a man in Scottish tartan who Peter thought he knew but was not sure and a lady. He recognised the lady vaguely but at first could not be sure. He closed his eyes, opened them again and refocussed.

Fiona! He must be dreaming. This could not be reality. He was aware of footsteps, arms around his neck, being smothered in kisses and the words; "Oh Peter, oh Peter. I thought you were dead. Of my lovely, wonderful man."

A deep Scottish accented voice sounded close by. "Now that's enough for now my dear. He is in deep shock, very unwell and he needs care and nurturing back to health. Leave it to the doctor. Your Peter is safe here," said the Duke of Argyll.

Peter's last recollection was the voice of the Duke. Then he fell asleep from the injection the doctor had given him.

CHAPTER

20

Downstairs in the Duke of Argyll's private rooms, Constable McCullan was emailing a detailed report to Police Scotland HQ in Glasgow. When he had been initially called to the Castle by the Duke he had been told over the phone that two of the Duke's Estate workers had found Peter at the side of one of the hillside tracks used by deer stalkers and had immediately radioed in so that the search for Peter could be called off.

But surely this was only part of the story? He would have to be patient and wait for Peter to come to and be able to give a more detailed account of what had happened.

Back at Tyndrum, police enquiries had revealed the identity of two cars seen parked by the white cottages. A search of the nearby town of Crianlarich had revealed the car and two men had been taken in for questioning. They had EU passports and claimed they lived in The Netherlands but Police Scotland had reason to believe they were indeed fake. Enquiries were continuing.

At Fort Willam, Alistair had been taken, under caution, from The

Highland hotel to the local police station as it had been reported it was his car seen at the white cottages. To begin with he denied it had been him, then changed his story several times before admitting to the police he might have been parked there while he went across the road to the little general store.

The Police needed more evidence and to link him with any particular crime.

He was released on bail pending further enquiries.

Back at Inverary Castle Peter had recovered sufficiently to be allowed to sit up in bed and answer questions. A team of specialist officers from Glasgow had driven up to question him. The Duke of Argyll had personally welcomed them and tea and biscuits were provided.

Fiona had been allowed to remain in Peter's bedroom during the questioning, having explained to the senior officer, a Chief Superintendent, the connection between her and Peter.

"Why did you go to those white cottages Mr Kingston," he was asked.

"Why did you think there was a connection between jewellery shop raids in England and the Tyndrum gold mine?"

Peter started to get his mind into gear. To cast his mind back and recollect everything that had happened.

He started to outline his theory that an international gang of thieves, only interested in gold, had been working across England. "But I had no evidence. It was just one of those gut feelings and when I encountered the Dutch coach and driver first at Loch Achray, then at Fort William, and then later at the Green Wellie shop at Tyndrum and they were speaking with the Highland Hotel Manager, Alistair, I began to have suspicions," said Peter.

The Chief Superintendent said he understood Peter had been in Scotland purely to write travel articles featuring the Lochs and Glens hotels so why had he not simply stuck to doing that?

Peter explained that he had been fascinated by his visit to the Tyndrum gold mine; that the Dutch coach driver and courier had not seemed who they claimed to be. He told the Chief Superintendent. "I am sure in your job, as well as mine as a news journalist, that sometimes things do not always ring true. To me there was something about these people that was not right and when I saw them at Tyndrum carrying a wheel hub cap and then seeing what they were doing in the tunnel with hub caps, well that just convinced me."

Yes, Mr Kingston. "I need to come to this tunnel and what you witnessed in a moment but tell me about the hub cap," said the chief superintendent.

"Well, I saw them emerging from one of the white cottages carrying this large hub cap and then fitting it to the coach in the Green Wellie car park. At the time it seemed odd. Then, when I was in the tunnel beneath the end cottage, I saw three men pouring what appeared to be liquid gold into the rim and when it had cooled, they sprayed the inside with some dark spray paint," said Peter.

The policemen looked at each other. "You are convinced it was gold," asked the senior officer.

"As sure as I could be. It had crossed my mind that they must be melting down the items of gold jewellery that had been stolen. This must be how they are getting the gold out of the country," said Peter.

At that moment, the door opened and in came the doctor. He did not look best pleased.

He addressed the senior officer and said in his opinion his patient had not yet fully recovered and was strong enough to face intensive questioning and he must insist that Peter Kingston be given more time to recover.

The officer said they had a job to do, and it was important to establish as much evidence as possible in order to apprehend the international jewellery thieves.

"One more question, Mr Kingston. How did you get into the tunnel and why?" he was asked.

Peter explained what had happened. The fact he had seen the Manager of the Highland Hotel in the lane outside the end white cottage as he was looking around inside. "I saw this trap door, quickly went down the ladder pulling it shut behind me. Heavy items were placed on top of the trap door preventing me from getting back out."

"What did you do?" asked the officer.

Peter outlined how he had made his way along the tunnel using is mobile phone torch until the battery was exhausted. Dim lights had come on; he saw this group of men gathered around a pot over a very hot fire and they then appeared to be pouring a liquid from the pot, which they loaded from many suitcases.

The officer and his colleague were looking more and more intrigued.

"I am guessing but I thought it was liquid gold," said Peter.

An intake of breath from the policemen. "What happened next?" asked the senior officer.

Peter explained how he had fallen asleep and when he woke up the light had gone out. How he made his way along the wall and then when the tunnel ended how he made his way back on the opposite side until the dim lights came back on; three men came along another tunnel but he was sufficiently hidden not to be seen.

Peter explained that despite feeling weak, wet and cold, he made his way along that tunnel feeling fresh air until he came to an entrance and was out, not knowing where he was. How he had discovered the wooden cabin, nearly got caught grabbing some bread and how he had hidden in the forest.

"You were very fortunate the Duke of Argyll's estate workers found you when they did. You might have died from exposure," said the officer.

He then explained to Peter that that officials from the Home Office in London, together with HM Customs and Excise officers, were on their way by plane from London to Glasgow and would then travel to Inveraray and the Duke's castle to interview him further.

Fiona asked. "Is this all really necessary? Peter is still weak, recovering from the horrific ordeal and just needs rest and quiet."

The officer said it was vitally important the international gang of jewellery thieves were caught.

With that, he thanked Peter and thanked the Duke of Argyll on his way out of the castle.

A bowl of warm broth was brought to Peter. The doctor reappeared and checked Peter over.

"You have had a very lucky escape," said the doctor. "No lasting damage done but you will need to continue to rest and regain your strength. It will be three or four days before you are fit to travel," he said.

Several hours later an official looking car swept into the castle's private driveway and after a discussion with the Duke of Argyll, several men in dark grey suits came into Peter's bedroom.

One of the men who introduced himself as an official from the Home Office, apologised to Peter for disturbing him but explained how important it was to discover what Peter could tell them about the men he had seen both at the Green Wellie café and below ground in then tunnel leading from the white cottages.

"We have a team of officers working with Police Scotland searching the tunnels as we speak. Another group of officers believe they have found the log cabin who have already described, and a search is taking place there," he said.

"Mr Kingston. "What led you to believe there was a connection between the various jewellery shop raids and the Tyndrum gold mine?" he asked.

Peter again repeated that it was just a hunch after he discovered there was a real gold mine in the Scottish Highlands. "Police throughout England did not seem to be establishing any clues to link each of the jewellery shop raids. I had nothing to go on until I met those suspicious Dutch tourist coach drivers," Peter told him. "I still do not believe they are Dutch at all."

"We tend to agree with you and police and immigration officers at various ports have been alerted to stop any Dutch coaches before they board ferries," he told Peter.

"The men detained in the Crianlarich car park with Dutch registered cars are still being questioned but we believe they may have connections to Albania," said the Home Office official.

"Crikey," exclaimed Peter.

He explained to Peter that several small items of jewellery had been found down the side of the passenger seat in the car. "Probably fell out of someone's pocket without them realising," he said.

"We are awaiting news from Police Scotland at Fort William where they have been questioning the manager of the Highland hotel. I think he knows more than he has been willing to admit up until now."

Peter said he thought the manager who he knew as Alistair was probably just a small cog in a big wheel. "He did not strike me as a real criminal and the last time I saw him with the men he seemed to be arguing about something," commented Peter.

"That's as maybe," Mr. Kingston. "We have to keep an open mind at this stage. "The various Agencies involved are just curious to know how the jewellery shop thieves managed to pull off each of the shop raids without leaving any apparent clues. It was not until the shop raid at Moffat that dashcam footage gave Police Scotland a lead."

Peter was feeling especially tired now. The questions had really taxed him, and the doctor came back in the room telling the officials it was time for them to leave.

"Yes, we understand and you have been quite helpful Mr Kingston. Thank you. "Once statements have been obtained from the hotel manager at Fort William we might have more of an insight into what has been going on. But you will be kept informed. Thank you for your help."

With that, the group of men departed and apologised to the Duke of Argyll on their way out for the disturbance.

Fiona came over to Peter's bedside, held his hand and whispered.

"It seems you have been right all along, Peter. Your hunch about gold mines and jewellery thefts were linked, if not directly with the Tyndrum gold mine. By the way, Peter your Editor was on the phone earlier. I had your mobile put on charge and when it rang, I answered and introduced myself and told your Editor what was happening. He seemed very pleased you were ok and that it had not been your fault directly," she told Peter.

"However, Peter, he did ask me to ensure you stopped poking around at holes in the ground which were none of your business and to tell you he was giving you a further seven days Leave of Absence to recover," said Fiona smiling.

"We might manage that short break together after all" whispered Peter. And with that he fell into a deep dreamless sleep.

CHAPTER

21

At the Fort William police station Alistair caved in and said. "I want to turn Queen's evidence".

The officer said they could not make any deals or promises but if he provided information helpful to the police in tracking down the jewellery gang it could stand him in good stead.

Alistair outlined how he had originally become involved, quite innocently, by agreeing to collect a suitcase which a Dutch coach driver said they had forgotten to pick up. He had kept it in the boot of his car until he had met up with them over a month previously at the Green Wellie shop and café.

The driver and courier had opened it in front of him and taken several photos showing Alistair with a suitcase containing gold jewellery and had threatened to "spill the beans" to both his employers and Police Scotland if he said anything.

"Was this a one-off, Sir" asked the police officer.

Alistair told them he had collected several suitcases on a number of occasions from various locations and then handed them over at the Green

Wellie café.

"I did not know at the time they owned the white cottages. It was only later when they said I should accompany them with the suitcase that I realised I had become involved in jewellery thefts. When I read about the jewellery raid at Moffat and the shop owner had been tied up and gagged that I told them I wanted nothing more to do with them," said Alistair.

"They showed me the coach wheel hub caps and said they contained melted down gold which was then sprayed so it was not obvious if anyone inspected it. I told them I would leave the last two suitcases at the cottage and that would be an end to things," he said.

The officer then asked Alistair if he had known Peter Kingston was hiding in the cottage cellar and that by placing the heavy suitcases on top of the trap door it had prevented Peter from getting out.

"I honestly had no idea Peter Kingston was down there. I liked him very much when he came to the hotel and although I thought it was suspicious he was hanging around Tyndrum, I did not know he had gone into the end cottage," said Alistair.

"Is Peter Kingston ok?" he added.

"Yes, he was found on the moorland having found his own way out of the tunnel," said the officer.

"Did you know the tunnel was being used for melting down all the stolen gold," he again asked.

"Certainly not," replied Alistair. "I knew it was happening because of the hub caps but I have personally never been in the tunnel."

He was asked how many people he thought might be involved in the theft or gold.

"It must be quite a few but again I do not know," said Alistair.

The officer asked if he knew they were not Dutch.

"I guessed they were not because other people from The Netherlands I have met in the past have all been very nice. I even met some of the passengers when they came to The Highland Hotel and they were lovely, genuine Dutch people. But there were several of the coach drivers and the couriers who were definitely not Dutch sounding. But they had Dutch passports," said Alistair.

The senior officer decided to leave the questioning there for now and he told Alistair he would be released on Police Bail pending further enquiries.

"I think, Sir, you should get yourself a solicitor as you will probably have to appear in court at some stage," said the officer. "I am not saying there will be charges, but best be prepared."

Alistar thanked him and left, relieved it was all over. Well, over for now. What charges might he face?

Back at Tyndrum several dozen police officers from various parts of The Highlands were involved in searching the two white cottages and some, equipped with powerful lamps, had gone into the tunnel.

With the aid of the copies of maps of very old mine workings supplied by The Duke of Argyll, police had managed to work out approximately where the tunnel might reappear. Using a robust Land Rover a group had followed the original track towards the Tyndrum gold mine, then turned right which led between two of the highest hills and eventually came to the forest. A brief search along the edge of the trees revealed the log cabin. Parking some distance away, four of the officers approached on foot.

Inside were two men unaware of what had been happening. They were arrested and handcuffed and to the amazement of the officers a large number of bottles of Tyndrum Gold Whisky were discovered in the back room. But not only the whisky. Boxes and boxes of souvenirs ranging from hand-sized models of "Nessie" – the legendary Loch Ness monster and six large wheel hub caps.

The police called for reinforcements as they would not be able to transport the arrested men and the haul of items.

Eventually, a large police van occupied by an inspector and two more officers arrived to take the arrested men away. The men were refusing to answer any questions.

The Inspector was amazed at the haul found in the log cabin. He knew from having heard about wheel hub caps being made with gold and then coloured over to avoid the detection but why bottles of Tyndrum Gold Whisky? This was normally only sold from the Green Wellie shop.

He radioed in with the news.

At the Green Wellie car park, Police Scotland had set up an "Incident HQ" and visitors were amazed at what was going on. But when anyone approached a police officer for answers, they were given the same answer "We are making enquiries into a very serious incident and at this stage cannot say more."

The team of Home Office, Immigration and Special Branch men had arranged for all those arrested to be taken to Glasgow for further questioning. Translators had been brought in just in case those arrested only wanted to answer questions – if at all – in Dutch or Albanian.

In the tunnel other police officers had found a quantity of gas bottles and a number of moulds. There was a suitcase still containing gold bracelets, gold watch straps and gold rings. The large pot used for melting down gold items was also in one corner. Quite a large-scale operation had been happening here. All the items were recorded, labelled and carefully moved back along the tunnel to the ladder which led down from the end white cottage.

Back at the Duke of Argyll's castle, Peter and Fiona were discussing the next few days. The doctor had told them Peter would be strong enough in two days' time to leave so where should they go? Peter decided he would have to contact his Editor, Bert, and say he would be delayed by a few days.

Peter knew his Editor would not be best pleased with him. After all, he had been told not to get involved in mines and gold. Well, this was slightly different, thought Peter, trying to convince himself nothing had been his fault.

After all, now that the whole story was coming out, had it not been for him, the gold smuggling gang might not have been discovered? Well, he had convinced himself if nobody else!

His mobile rang on the other side of the room. Fiona answered it.

"Peter. It's your Editor who would like a few words."

Oh crikey, thought Peter. Was he for the high jump?

"Hello Peter. How are you?" asked Bert. "Seems from the phone calls I have been getting from the police, Home Office, Immigration and others, you have managed to crack an international gang of gold smugglers. I suppose I should give you a severe ticking off for doing everything I told you not to. But I know about your nose for a good story, the trouble is it seems to get you into trouble. Then you come out of it smelling of roses," said Bert with a slight chuckle.

He told Peter that whilst the original plan was for Peter to return from Scotland on Monday, a few extra days to completely recover might be in order.

"I understand a very nice young lady might have taken your fancy and from what the Duke of Argyll told me yesterday, you are a very lucky young man to have found yourself such a lady who also played her part in ensuring you were found. Enjoy the extra days and I will see you here at the office in a week's time," said Bert.

Fiona said she was going to drive back to her home and spend a few hours with her mother. "I also need to speak to my boss at the Enterprise car hire office at Glasgow Airport and arrange a few extra days leave. But do not worry, Peter. I will be back here in the morning."

With that, she gave Peter a long, lingering kiss and embrace and then was gone.

A short time later the Duke of Argyll visited, to confirm Peter's progress.

"Hello Peter. The doctor says you are making good progress. No doubt, something to do with that delightful young lady who obviously thinks a great deal about you," said the Duke.

Peter told him how grateful he was for the Duke allowing him to recover at the castle. "I only hope that one day gold might be discovered somewhere on your estate – but legal gold and not items stolen from jewellery shops said Peter, smiling.

"It is funny you should say that, Peter, as a result of making those all maps of mines available to the police, geologists have asked permission to come and do fresh surveys of the rock strata in an around those old lead mine tunnels. I am told there is a possibility that other mineral deposits such as silver and perhaps traces of gold could be there somewhere. After all, the Tyndrum gold mine is not a million miles away from some of the lead mine tunnels which lead towards my estate and why should they only exist at Tyndrum?" said the Duke.

This gave Peter an idea which for the moment he would keep to himself. First, he and Fiona needed to spend a few days somewhere quiet together before he boarded that train from Glasgow Central back to London and reality. He was really going to miss the beauty of the Scottish Highlands, not to mention Fiona.

Something must be done!

The next day, having thanked the Duke of Argyll again for his kindness and informed Police Scotland that he would be available at the end of his mobile phone, Peter and Fiona left the castle. She told him that his suitcase and laptop were safely in the boot of her car. "Your Enterprise car has been collected and taken back to the Airport depot," she told him.

Fiona had been in touch with the hotel on Loch Lomond where they had originally intended to stay a few days ago. The hotel management had been very understanding and, yes, a room with a view of Loch Lomond was still available.

Having checked in after an uneventful journey with Fiona at the wheel, they went to their room and fondly embraced for an age. "Oh Peter, please never leave me again. I am so deeply in love with you and thinking of what might have happened to you last week made me realise how much you have come to mean to me," said Fiona.

Peter looked into her eyes, gripped her hands firmly and said he felt the same.

"But you do realise I have to return to my newspaper in a few days' time. I shall miss you and will try and get back here as soon as I can. Tomorrow, I have a small surprise for you," he said.

"Oh, tell me now Peter, please Peter."

He was adamant. "No, wait until tomorrow, Fiona, otherwise it will not be a surprise," he said.

So after a shower, they went down to dinner and enjoyed a traditional dinner and some red wine.

Back in the room, they snuggled up together in a warm, lasting cuddle which they had been unable to do at the castle. Peter had never felt like this before. How could be concentrate on his work back in Surrey leaving this lovely girl behind in Scotland.

The next morning after breakfast Peter suggested he drive, and they went through the beautiful Scottish countryside and eventually came out at the town of Callander. Peter parked in the main street, looked across at Fiona and said, "Ever since I first met you I have become more and more fond of you. Now I am beyond fond and so much in love with you I do not know what life could possibly hold without you. So, my wonderful, lovely Fiona, would you agree to marry me?"

Fiona burst into tears, fell across the front passenger seat and wrapped her arms around Peter's neck.

"Yes please Peter. Oh Peter. How wonderful. I promise to always make you happy too, my darling man."

"That's settled then. Now for the surprise." He came round to the passenger door and held it open while Fiona got out. Hand in hand they walked a short distance to a local jewellery shop and once inside, told the owner. "I would like an engagement ring for this lovely lady please."

Fiona just could not believe it. The jewellery shop owner produced several trays of rings, and it took an age before Fiona finally settled on a design. Trying it on it would need a slight adjustment but the owner assured Peter it could be ready later that day.

"You have chosen something a bit special, young lady, he told Fiona. The ring is made from Scottish gold mined from the gold mine at Tyndrum."

Peter and Fiona looked at each other and both burst out laughing. It was sometime before they were able to explain to the man what was so funny.

"You are surely not the young man found on the moorland, not the young man who has led the police to the international jewellery gang behind all those raids. Oh, goodness me. And here you are in my shop. Well, the Tyndrum gold ring will surely remind you for the rest of your days together of this adventure," he said.

Peter and Fiona left the shop promising to be back later to collect the ring.

"Let's go and have a cup of coffee and we had better phone your Mother and you can tell her the news," said Peter.

Fiona's Mother was overjoyed. "Peter is such a lovely young man, but you have many things to sort out first. Where will you live when you are married?" Fiona told her mother just one step at a time.

"I am as surprised as you are Mother. "I had no idea what Peter had planned until a short time ago. Peter and I will spend the coming days discussing all these things. I am just so, so excited," said Fiona.

The next couple of days were idyllic. Love-making; just being together. Holding hands and strolling along the shore of Loch Lomond. Fiona asked Peter what he thought to the idea that she moved south. "There are Enterprise car hire offices close to where you live and I am sure I could apply for a transfer," said Fiona.

Peter told her she had to be absolutely sure she wanted to leave the beautiful western Highlands and really the only life she had known so far. "After all, and please do not think I am trying to discourage you, but the south of England is a busy, bustling place with lots of people and noise. Totally the opposite of what you have been used to," said Peter.

"If I did not know you better Peter Kingston I would think you are trying to put me off," said Fiona laughing. "I just want to be near you, wherever you are living," she said.

Peter said he had already given it some thought and maybe, just maybe, he might prefer at some stage in the not too distant future to be living in Scotland. "After all, you have newspapers and some very good ones. Maybe I do not want to contemplate the hustle and bustle of everyday life in the south for ever more," said Peter.

"But there is no rush. We have to set a date for the wedding and whether it will be here or down south," said Peter. "Traditionally it is usually where the bride comes from and I am sure your mother would like it to be here in Scotland," he said.

They both agreed to think about it and soon; far too soon Peter would be heading back south by train. "Let's just enjoy our time together and hope it will not be too long before you can return to visit me," said Fiona.

Their last night together was passionate. Very little talking other than constant reminding each other what the other meant. "I cannot believe it has happened so suddenly, but I know for sure it is all that I want," Peter told Fiona.

The dreaded morning arrived, and Fiona drove Peter into the heart of Glasgow and they parked near the Central railway station. Holding hands with his laptop slung over his shoulder Peter gripped Fiona's hand tightly until they arrived at his carriage door. He had a reserved window seat. They were still embracing and kissing passionately when the guard blew his whistle and the door had to close.

Peter promised to phone her when he got to London and speak to his Editor about how soon he could take some proper leave!

Fiona was still waving as the 12-coach train pulled out of Glasgow and rounded the bend over the river Clyde.

He had just got himself comfortable when his mobile phone rang.

"Hello Peter. It's Argyll, Duke of. News travels fast here in The Highlands and I have just heard you have got yourself engaged to be married to that lovely young lady."

"Yes, your Grace. She has made me a very happy man."

"Well Peter. It is never too early to start planning and when it comes to a wedding venue, I would like to offer my castle as a possible venue. All at my expense," said the Duke.

"That is so very kind of you. I will let Fiona know. I am sure her mother would be happy to know the wedding would take place here in The Highlands. Thank you," said Peter.

Eventually after a fast journey of just over four hours from Glasgow the train pulled into Euston and as he crossed the concourse Peter noticed a newspaper vendor and a poster claiming. "Albanian Jewel Theft Gang Held".

Peter purchased a newspaper and as he sat in the back heading towards his train down to Reigate, Peter read that Immigration and HM Customs officials had seized a coach at Felixstowe believed to have concealed gold on board. Cases of whisky bottles marked Tyndrum Gold had been stored in a side panel of the coach. When a bottle had been opened, concealed inside was a cigar-shaped tube of what appeared to be solid gold. Tests were to be carried out.

Boxes of souvenirs were also found in the coach. Some were thought to be made of gold, others were thought to have been packed with gold. It was believed the gold had formed part of the many gold jewellery thefts and the items melted down in a tunnel in The Highlands of Scotland. A young English journalist was thought to have assisted Police Scotland in finding the gold jewellery.

Meanwhile over in The Netherlands, Dutch police had raided a house near Rotterdam and arrested five Albanian men believed to be ringleaders in a gold smuggling ring responsible for numerous jewellery shop raids throughout the UK.

Ah well, thought Peter, that all sounds very positive.

A taxi took him from the Reigate railway station to his newspaper office. He went straight to Bert's office, knocked, went in and Bert looked up. "Ah, there you are Peter. Good to see you back."

"How do you fancy covering a garden show at the weekend. I believe there is a nice silver cup for the Best in Show winner. Sorry it's not gold."

And as a parting shot, Bert called out. "By the way, many congratulations on your engagement. If you promise not to do anything more adventurous than put a gold ring on the girl's finger, I might arrange for you to have some time off for a honeymoon!"

Peter closed his editor's door and smiling, said to himself. "Nice to be back in the real world."

THE END

ABOUT THE AUTHOR

The Author was born in Dover and educated at boarding school in Canterbury and then at college at Wigan, Lancashire. With an ambition since early teenage years of being a journalist, Paul returned to the south of England and landed a five-year apprenticeship with the County Newspaper of Kent. He spent four years at the Journalist Training College before moving to another regional newspaper and worked his way up to being a District Manager and then to East Kent News Editor.

Paul then spent some time with the BBC Southeast Radio in London before doing a four-year course in Public Relations.

He was appointed Director of Communications, HM Submarines, Gosport, but before taking up this appointment he was offered – and accepted – the role of taking charge of the Press and Public Relations department at the Port of Dover. He later became Corporate Affairs Manager and spent nearly 20 years with the Port Authority before taking early retirement to look after his wife of 40 years who had become seriously ill with Terminal Cancer.

During his writing career Paul has written numerous books including many editions of Drive Right Into Europe and Ski Drive. He developed his own skiing website which became the largest and most comprehensive in Europe.

Following the death of his wife, Paul turned his writing to producing Novels and this latest book is a sequel to The Powder Man. Now a third in the trilogy involving his central character is planned for later this year.